"Why  he p...........

Dare could feel his gray eyes watching her. "Besides the disenchantment," he went on.

"Isn't that enough?" she asked quietly. The sight of the gemlike lake, the peaceful vineyards, reminded her of how complex her life had become yet how simple it should be.

"Not around here." His hand held hers and it felt hard, alive with strength. "On top of the mountain we don't allow disenchantment. Only enchantment, pure and simple."

His gaze moved disconcertingly between her lips and eyes. "You know," he said, smiling, "you've got a funny face. A pretty, funny face—as if you don't know how pretty you are."

Dare met his gaze and her heart gave an unwanted little flip and she felt warm with a heat the August sun hadn't created.

Bethany Campbell, an English major, teacher and textbook consultant, calls her writing world her "hidey-hole," that marvelous place where true love always wins out. Her hobbies include writing poetry and thinking about that little scar on Harrison Ford's chin. She laughingly admits that her husband, who produces videos and writes comedy, approves of the first one only.

Books by Bethany Campbell

HARLEQUIN ROMANCE
2726—AFTER THE STARS FALL
2779—ONLY A WOMAN
2803—A THOUSAND ROSES
2815—SEA PROMISES

HARLEQUIN INTRIGUE
65—PROS AND CONS

Don't miss any of our special offers. Write to us at the following address for information on our newest releases.

Harlequin Reader Service
901 Fuhrmann Blvd., P.O. Box 1397, Buffalo, NY 14240
Canadian address: P.O. Box 603,
Fort Erie, Ont. L2A 5X3

The Long Way Home

Bethany Campbell

Harlequin Books

TORONTO • NEW YORK • LONDON
AMSTERDAM • PARIS • SYDNEY • HAMBURG
STOCKHOLM • ATHENS • TOKYO • MILAN

ISBN 0-373-02852-0

Harlequin Romance first edition August 1987

CHAPTER ONE

IT WAS RAINING, and the flashbulbs were blinding her.

"Sheffy!" screamed one of the reporters. "Where's Sullivan? Why isn't he here?"

"Sheffy! This way! Look this way!" cried a photographer.

"Where's Sullivan? Does this mean things have changed between you two?" another voice called out.

Warren and the chauffeur guided her through the cemetery gates, trying to shield her.

The chauffeur elbowed a newsman who got too close, then swore at the pack of them. "Leave the girl alone. She just came from her mother's burial, you cretins."

He swore again and helped Dare into the back of the limousine.

How odd, she thought numbly. She was being protected by a man she didn't even know. The chauffeur had been provided by the funeral home.

"Vultures!" the chauffeur said angrily to the press corps, as he hurried Warren into the car and slammed the door.

Warren glowered at him. "Who does he think he is?" he asked Dare grumpily. "Prince Valiant? Rule number one: if you ain't royalty, don't insult the press."

She said nothing. She stared down at her hands in the black gloves.

"Where's Sullivan?" yelled a photographer, as the long black car pulled away. "Sheffy! Honey! Where's lover-boy?" he persisted.

"I could kill Sullivan," Warren huffed, lighting a cigar. "The little bleached-blond rat. It doesn't look good, him not showing up. This is going to take some explaining. If Fawn was alive, she'd give him a piece of her mind as big as Long Island."

"Fawn's not alive," Dare said, her voice toneless. "That's the whole point." Fawn—her mother, her brilliant, charming, relentless mother—was dead. Dare couldn't cry yet. Not yet.

"Yeah," said Warren, puffing hard to start the cigar. "Sorry." He looked out the window of the limo. "Rotten day. Rotten. Sorry, kid."

The rain poured down.

Dare leaned her forehead against the window. She was a tall girl, too slender. Her dark brown eyes looked both haunted and hunted. Her overly generous mouth was taut. She had lovely high cheekbones and a slightly tip-tilted nose, and she always wore full makeup in public, as she had been trained to do.

She was only nineteen, but she was exhausted. Her long honey-blond hair was pulled back so severely that her temples hurt. She was wearing her best earrings—the sapphires—because her mother would have wanted her to.

"You wearing your engagement ring?" Warren asked.

She stripped the glove from her left hand without emotion. It was bare.

"No," Dare said dispassionately. "I took it off."

"So put it back on," Warren said wearily. "Maybe we should be glad Sullivan didn't show. You'd have got mobbed worse than you did." He sighed, exhaling a cloud of smoke. He was a small, round man with a fringe of slick black hair. A former banker, he had been her business manager for seven years.

"I'm not putting it back on," she said, her tone impassive. "He didn't come to see her when she was sick. Not once. We'd go out on those stupid publicity dates, and I'd try to talk to him about it but he wouldn't. He told me he didn't want to talk about it. It was too depressing."

"Sheffy, he's an artist. He's temperamental. Let's forget it. We'll figure out a way to explain it. I'm sorry I brought it up."

"He's not an artist," she replied. "He's a rock singer." She paused for a moment staring out at the rain. "He never came to see her, even once. And don't call me 'Sheffy.' My name's Dareen."

"Your name is Sheffy. It's a million-dollar name. I said I'm sorry I brought the whole thing up. So he didn't come see her. What was to see? She was practically comatose from that first stroke. For three months she couldn't say a word. She wouldn't have wanted him to see her anyway. Not to insult the dead, but she was a vain woman. Where's the ring?"

She didn't answer. She watched the rain beating against the window.

"Sheffy," he said anxiously. "I'm your business manager. My job is to protect your interests. Now, where's the ring? You didn't give it back, did you?"

"Why would I give it back?" she asked, her face tense. "Fawn bought it. Out of the publicity budget. It belongs to us." She winced, remembering that Fawn was gone and there was no more "us." For three months she had sat at Fawn's bedside, not believing that such a force of personality could be slowed or stilled.

"Put it back on tomorrow," Warren ordered. "You've got an engagement that's worth a fortune in publicity to you—and Sullivan, too. You're not gonna break it off on a whim."

"It's hardly a whim. And it was never a real engagement," she replied, not looking at him. "Fawn came up with the whole idea."

"So? You liked him. You were crazy about him. I didn't hear any complaints."

"He never cared for me. He doesn't care about anything. Except himself and his career and his investments."

"He adores you. In his way."

"He adored Fawn. He knew how smart she was. They could sit and talk money all night long. He just put up with me, but he'd never be the right man for me. He should have come to see her. He should have."

"You're in a bad mood," Warren accused. "Let's not talk about it. We've got other things to talk about. Your career, for instance."

She turned and stared at him through her black mesh veil. "Warren—I don't want to talk about my career. My mother just died. Remember?"

Warren grunted slightly. "Yeah? Well, excuse my lack of sentiment, but your mother was one hard-nosed lady. And what else would she want you to be talking about? Be realistic, Sheffy. It's not like Fawn's dying was a shock or anything. We knew it was gonna happen. Be thankful that—"

"I know," she said tiredly, turning to look at the rain again. "Be thankful that she didn't suffer longer. Well I am thankful. But I don't want to talk business."

"Your career was her life," Warren persisted. "You think you got to be a top model from sheer dumb luck?

Think again. She built it—the whole image. And now you've got to go it alone. You've got some serious decisions to make. We've got investments to discuss. Frankly, the way she wanted your trust managed was not such a good idea. I'm going to have to do some fancy footwork. To tell the truth—"

"Please, Warren." She leaned her forehead against the window again. The cool glass felt soothing.

"Sheffy," he insisted, "believe me. Fawn would want us to be talking about this. You've got things to decide."

"I'll think about them later." She closed her eyes.

Warren gave up all pretense of being a mourner. His voice was businesslike and harsh. "You better think about them now. Look. You're in a unique position. You're at the top of the heap. You're the *numero uno* model in New York. You've got mystique. You're nineteen years old. There's no place you couldn't go. But you've gotta be careful. You've gotta plan. Now that Fawn's gone, you need a publicist. I was thinking of Sullivan's. He's good. He's aggressive."

She didn't bother to open her eyes. "Sullivan's publicist? Good grief, Warren. I don't believe this. I'm having a bad dream."

"You and Sullivan are a dynamite combination. It makes sense."

"Sullivan and I are no combination at all. It was all make-believe. Everything about my life is make-believe."

Warren made a noise of disgust. " 'My whole life is make-believe,' " he mocked. "Now you're going melodramatic on me. You've got everything in the world a girl could want, kid. Fawn got it for you. You want to hang on to it? Then listen to me."

Suddenly her head ached. Her whole life seemed insane, pointless, unreal. She opened her dark eyes and faced him again. "Whoever said I wanted everything in the world? Whoever said I even wanted to be a model?"

"Fawn did," he said, regarding her over the glowing tip of his fat cigar. "And who do you know that ever said no to Fawn? Nobody, that's who. Not you, not me, not Sullivan, not anybody."

"I want to go away for a while," Dare said, looking out the window again.

"All right. We talk a few things over, then you can take a week off. Go to Bar Harbor. Go to Cape Ann."

"Longer than a week. A year."

"A year?" Warren's voice rose nearly to a shriek. "You crazy? Where would you go for a year? You know what kind of money you could lose in a year?"

"I canceled everything when Mama—when Fawn got sick. I've got no appointments."

"I recall," he said sourly. "Excuse the references, but she's probably already turning in her brand new grave over that."

"I'm going south," she uttered, almost to herself. "Just—down south."

"The South?" Warren asked, aghast. "As in Dixie and all that grits and gravy schtick?"

She nodded mechanically.

"Sheffy, Fawn fought and scratched like a cat to get you and her *out* of the South and to where you are today."

"And today I'm in a funeral car, Warren. I said I'm leaving. I've already made arrangements."

He stared at her as if she had announced she were taking vows and joining a convent.

"Get serious," he ordered.

"It's where we started from. I'm going back."

He swore softly. "You mean it, don't you?"

She nodded numbly.

He shook his head, disbelief in his eyes. "I see it. I see it for the first time," he said, disgustedly.

She looked at him questioningly.

"I see her in your face. I always wondered how she ever had a kid like you—such a patient, nice, innocent, cooperative kid. All of a sudden, I see her in you. You really mean it, don't you?" he repeated. "You don't care what it does to anybody. You're actually gonna leave."

She nodded again. "I have to. For a while. It's all got so crazy. Maybe it always was crazy, and I was just too naive to realize it. I just never knew anything else."

"You can't do this," he said, getting ready to fight her. "What about Sullivan?"

She thought about that for a moment. She had been in love with Sullivan—or she thought she had, which amounted to the same thing. She'd had a crush on him from the time she was seventeen. Their so-called romance was one of the most publicized in America. Except it wasn't really a romance. Sullivan kissed her only when photographers were looking on.

"If Sullivan wants me badly enough, I suppose he'll come after me," she said. In a way she hoped he might.

"You're crazy." Warren shook his balding head. "You're nineteen years old. You know nothing. You've always been taken care of. Fawn told you when to sneeze, for God's sake. She told you when to wipe your nose. You can't just go off alone."

Dare didn't listen. She was going away. Her mind was made up.

"Listen," Warren said desperately. "At least promise me you won't break the engagement. If you won't think of your career, think of Sullivan's."

She nodded wearily. "Just no more publicity about it for a while," she pleaded. "I won't break it. But please, let it die a natural death. No publicity, all right? Promise? He doesn't need me. He never did."

At last Warren nodded in reluctant agreement.

She stared at her slender, naked hand. Sometimes she wondered who she really was. She could barely remember a time when she hadn't been posing in front of a camera, pretending. Nothing about her life felt real—she was just an image.

"You know nothing." Warren was angry. "Nothing. I never met anybody who knew less. Fawn took all the lumps for you. She did all the fighting. You haven't the faintest idea what reality is. Sheffy? You listening to me?"

"My name is Dareen," she said.

ARCADIA said the sign at the city limits. In smaller print it said Population: 4,126 Nice Folks and A Few Old Grouches. And Some Darn Good Hound Dogs.

Dare smiled. Her dusty brown Chevrolet with its New York plates appeared to be the only car on the road. Arcadia—journey's end. Almost.

It was a hot Southern Saturday, late afternoon, and Arcadia seemed to be in some sort of enchanted doze. The mimosas lining Main Street stirred slightly, as if in a dreamy sleep. In the shade of the magnolia tree on the courthouse lawn slumbered a black-and-tan dog, presumably one of Arcadia's darn good hounds.

She slowed down. Across from the courthouse was the sign she'd been watching for:

McFee's Peerless Real Estate
Sales, Appraisals, Rentals
We Sell Root Worm Insurance!

She parked, got out of the car and stretched with happy weariness. She had driven almost seventeen hundred miles in the past three days. But it was worth it. She could almost feel the quiet, and it felt good.

She stretched again, running a hand through her long tawny hair. She tried to smooth her travel-wrinkled khaki shorts and white blouse, but with little success.

She set her oversize sunglasses more firmly on her nose and looked around at the languid town. It was as different from Manhattan as possible—just as she'd hoped it would be.

She opened the creaky door and walked into a musty office, where a ceiling fan droned lazily.

A thin, waspish man with a high-domed balding head looked up at her suspiciously from a garish tabloid. In spite of the heat he wore a black vest, tightly buttoned, and a narrow black necktie, tightly knotted.

The newspaper caught her attention. It made her instinctively grit her teeth. *Oh, no,* she thought.

"Grieving Model to Marry Rock Star at Last?" the headline asked shrilly.

She stopped in her tracks, suddenly nervous. She was glad she had no makeup on, that she looked ordinary and disheveled. Warren had promised he would stop the publicity on her and Sullivan. Apparently, he hadn't been able to stop this story.

The large cover picture showed Dare trying to hide her face from photographers. The bold-faced caption read, "Where Was Boyfriend when Beauty Buried Mom? See Page Six!"

Mr. McFee had apparently been seeing page six. He blinked up at Dare in obvious irritation, but gave no sign of recognizing her. Nervously, she took off her sunglasses. Without them she looked impossibly young and vulnerable.

Self-consciously she extended her hand to the man.

"Mr. McFee?" she asked. "I'm Dareen Sheffield." It was her real name, seldom used.

He gave a slight nod and took her hand, still peering up at her distrustfully. He was clearly not one of Arcadia's 4,126 nice folks.

"From New York," she continued, giving him as firm a handshake as possible. "We talked by phone. I'm renting the . . . Bailey farm, I think it is."

She hoped she sounded businesslike. She wasn't used to such dealings.

"Sheffield," he said. He had a squeaky, querulous voice. "Sheffield. Bailey farm. Yes. You're late. I expected you this morning."

"Tennessee is even longer than it looks on the map," she explained, smiling in apology.

"Tennessee is no better than it should be," he sniffed.

She hadn't the faintest idea what he meant by that and said nothing.

He studied her pointedly. "It's full of country and western singers who celebrate infidelity and drunkenness and truck stops," he said. "Nashville is full of painted women and grown men who wear rhinestones on their clothes and play country music on the guitar."

Dare blinked hard. She was still engaged, officially at least, to a man who wore rhinestones on his clothes and played the guitar. Sullivan didn't sing country and western, he played rock music, but Mr. McFee would doubtlessly think that was worse.

"From New York, you say?" he asked, squinting up at her. He fanned himself with the tabloid. He had folded it down the middle.

As if slightly hypnotized, Dare watched her own picture as the magazine moved back and forth.

"Yes." She almost whispered it.

"So what brings you to Arcadia?" he asked, frowning suspiciously.

"Nothing," she answered. She realized the answer sounded rude, so she added, "I had . . . there was a death in the family. I needed to get away for a while. Do some—"

She suddenly realized she didn't have a notion of what she intended to do, except to hide for a while, heal and, perhaps, find out what she really wanted from life.

"I need to do some thinking," she finished lamely.

"There's no money in thinking," Mr. McFee pronounced. "Perhaps we should talk about payment of rent in advance."

Dare sighed. "We can do more than talk about it," she said wearily.

Maybe Fawn had been right and everything in the world did come down to money. She took her purse from her shoulder and opened it. "I'll pay you now if you like. Are traveler's checks all right?"

"Sit down, sit down," said Mr. McFee, suddenly transformed into friendliness, or at least a close approximation of it.

Mr. McFee watched her sign the checks, then counted them carefully. "You realize I made you no promises about the state of the property?" he asked.

She nodded. "All I need is privacy and a view. On a mountain. A view where you can see a long way."

"That I can guarantee," he muttered. "If scenery was money, this state would be rich. And if you want any repairs done on the house, you pay for them."

"Fine."

"You're easily satisfied." His tone was contemptuous.

"I try to get along with people," she replied. That was true. She had always tried hard to please. Too hard, she now realized.

"I hope you know what you're getting into." He chuckled mirthlessly. "It's very isolated at that old farmhouse. You've only got one neighbor, and he's a bad lot. An odious man. But if you need any work done, you can call him for help. He owns that accursed winery."

"Winery?" Dare questioned, slightly surprised.

"DuLong Winery," Mr. McFee answered, as if he were saying bad words. "The biggest in the state."

She shrugged. She knew nothing about this region. After Fawn's death, she had gone home to the apartment and stuck a pin in the southern quadrant of a map of the United States. The point had pierced the paper right next to the small town of Arcadia. Nobody would ever find her.

"The lady you're renting from—Mrs. Bailey—doesn't approve of the DuLongs," the realtor said, shaking his balding head. "I don't either. The DuLongs have been after the Bailey property for years. To grow more grapes."

He said "grapes" with an expressive wrinkling of his long nose.

"Mr. DuLong will never get that property," he said piously. "Mrs. Bailey does not believe in fermented spirits. Nor do I. He who puts wine in his mouth puts in a thief to steal his wits. Mr. DuLong, in my opinion, is no better than a panderer to wine-bibbers and sots."

"Um," Dare said uncomfortably.

"Mr. Rupert DuLong has snapped up every other piece of ground in the area suitable for growing grapes," sniffed Mr. McFee. "He's exactly the sort of man you'd expect him to be. And I'll tell you something."

Mr. McFee leaned across his desk as if he were about to impart a secret too horrible to be uttered aloud.

"It isn't enough that he's forced all his neighbors to sell out," he whispered hoarsely, "or that he's a man of the most dissolute habits—especially where liquor and ladies are concerned. He's a confirmed playboy, a Don Juan of the worst sort. His parents' marriage was a miserable fiasco from the start. His mother was a helpless little thing who couldn't cope with that family of unprincipled hooch-mongers. She became a tranquilizer addict. I don't think she had a clear thought for the last ten years of her life. It's no wonder he hasn't an iota of respect for women."

Dare stirred in embarrassment. She didn't want to hear malicious gossip.

"Worse, the man has actually—" Mr. McFee's mouth narrowed in distaste "—the man has actually polluted the environment to the point where he has made the mockingbirds drunk!"

"He—what?" Dare said in surprise, her brown eyes widening. This was the sort of charge one didn't hear every day.

"He's poured the dregs of his wretched wine into the water system and actually got the mockingbirds drunk," Mr. McFee hissed, clearly horrified. "To say nothing of the possums and the quail and so forth. You have heard the saying 'drunk as a skunk'? Well, alas, on DuLong's

Mountain, the skunks *are* drunk. It's a scandal and an outrage. I am appalled. As are all right-thinking citizens.''

Dare sat silent, unsure what to say, her mind filled with images of inebriated mockingbirds flying headfirst into pine trees, while a quartet of drunken possums sang in barroom harmony.

"Nonetheless," said Mr. McFee briskly, "Mr. DuLong has a large staff of hirelings, and some are always grateful for an odd job. Should you need assistance, I'm sure one will be available. I would, however, make sure the man you hire is sober. It's well known most of them sample that witch's brew they make."

He tsked and tutted, then finally handed Dare the key to the farmhouse.

She rose and hurried toward the door. She had the feeling Mr. McFee was more than a little eccentric, and unpleasantly so.

"One more thing, Miss Sheffield," he called from his desk. She turned and looked at him. She was tired, and her dark eyes seemed larger, more defenseless than usual.

"You said you wanted a house with furniture. The house comes with furniture, as I said."

"Very good," she said, smiling stiffly. She turned to go again.

"The furniture, however, is not in the house. The last tenants had their own. The furniture has been stored in the barn. It's your responsibility to get it back to the house."

"Very good," she repeated, anxious to make her getaway. She was out the door before he could say more.

His words didn't sink in until she was well out of town, then she frowned, shaking her head in wonder. Her furniture was in the barn? The old grump had rented her a furnished house, but the furniture was in the barn? And her neighbor was a man who got mockingbirds drunk?

She smiled nervously. Maybe Warren was right; she wasn't capable of taking care of herself. She thought of her picture on the cover of the tabloid and stopped smiling. She willed herself to ignore that memory and all the others. She kept driving.

The oak and pine forests gave way to vineyards that seemed to unroll without limit from each side of the highway. An occasional billboard exhorted the tourist to visit Chateau DuLong, to taste the native wines and tour the cellars.

She passed through the tiny town of Dulong. Its sign announced Dulong, 300 Residents, but no grouches.

The Chevy rattled and shuddered as it climbed the steep grade out of the village. A sign informed her she was on Mount DuLong. The DuLong family must own half the county, she thought—maybe all the county except the forty acres she was renting.

Then she spotted the black mailbox that marked the graveled lane up to the Bailey farm. She willed the Chevy to make one last climb.

She finally reached the top of the mountain, and the sight before her was even lovelier than anything she'd imagined.

She parked the car by the huge old mulberry tree in the front yard and looked at the improbable little farmhouse. It was painted pale green, with garish yellow trim, and most of it seemed to be taken up by the front porch.

She got out of the car, no longer tired, but strangely exhilarated. The evening air was fresh and mellow. Somewhere a mockingbird sang. The sun was setting as she climbed the porch stairs. She looked toward the west and drew in her breath. The sky was turning into a sea of molten gold, and she could see for miles. Far below her a wide river glimmered golden in the sunset, and beyond it the mountains stretched, gilded and shadowed.

Gazing at the glowing sky and the sweep of the mountain-rimmed valley, she knew that what she had done, however instinctive, however irrational it had been, was right.

DARE SPENT THE WEEK mopping, scrubbing, polishing and patching. She attacked her tasks with elation. She was making a home for herself. For once in her life, things seemed genuine, not artificial.

"Illusion is the name of the game," Fawn had always taught her. After all these years, Dare delighted in the real, no matter how humble.

Her only bad moment had come when she'd walked into the back bedroom and found a former tenant had left a magazine photo of her taped to the wall.

She took it down. Somehow, photos of her face still had the power to surprise her. She never thought of herself as beautiful. Fawn had repeatedly told her she was not beautiful; she simply had a trick face—one that photographed well. That was all.

Beneath the picture was a rather breathless set of comments from the photographer.

"Gazelle eyes," he had rhapsodized. "Eyes of darkest innocence. That famous, plushy, sensuous mouth. With that all-knowing mouth and those unknowing eyes, what is she? Who is she? Temptress or child? Temptress *and* child?"

"She's the cleanup committee," Dare muttered, and threw the photo into a trash bag. She was glad to leave such nonsense behind. Even her long, unhappy romance with Sullivan was beginning to seem like a curious dream.

She had a real life here, with real problems—such as furniture. The farmhouse had only a stove and refrigerator and a few chairs she had managed to scrounge out of the old tumbledown red barn.

The barn was jammed with a thousand cast-offs. Mrs. Bailey, the owner, must have stored everything she didn't want there. A bizarre assortment of antiques and junk had been stacked haphazardly in the loft. There was an old love seat with purple upholstery, a hat rack of mounted moose antlers, and a lamp made out of a brass fire extinguisher.

There was no way she could get the love seat out of the hayloft by herself, or the mattress and springs and the bedframe. She was sleeping on the floor in the sleeping bag she had bought on her trip from New York. She felt like a pioneer, a survivalist. But she felt also like someone who was ready to sleep in a bed again. She drove to a pay phone in Dulong and called the winery to hire help.

"No problem," the receptionist assured her. "We'll send somebody as soon as possible. But it may be a few days. It's harvest time. But we're always glad to help. Welcome to the mountain."

DARE STOOD in the hayloft the next afternoon, mentally cataloging the furniture. How, she wondered, had anybody ever got the stuff up here in the first place?

She probably couldn't expect help from the winery until the next week. Well, she could get some small items down and improvise. She was becoming good at improvising.

The late-afternoon sunlight poured through the loft doors as she struggled with a mattress, but she couldn't move it. She would content herself with taking another small load to the house. As she stuffed the pockets of her shorts with dusty kitchen implements, she eyed the lamp made out of a fire extinguisher. She could use more light in the house. "All right, lamp," she said. "Down we go."

She hoisted it and was about to start down the loft ladder, but the lamp's dented shade made it awkward to handle. She unscrewed the shade, and rather than making two trips she put it on her head. She picked up the lamp in one arm and started gingerly down the ladder.

She felt completely ridiculous and perversely enjoyed it. For the past week she had gloried in not looking glamorous. Besides, she thought wryly, the lamp shade probably looked better than some of the avant-garde fashions she had modeled.

She reached the bottom at last, her arms shaking from the effort. She turned and headed toward the barn door.

"Now that," said a deep and lazy voice far too close to her, "is the darnedest thing I've ever seen. But I must admit, you did it with style. Great style."

She whirled with a gasp. She hugged the lamp closer to her, as if for protection.

A tall man with very long muscular legs stood in front of her. He wore faded jeans and a sweat-stained blue-and-white sports jersey. He had thick, wind-rumpled brown hair, and an easy, amused smile curved his upper lip. He leaned casually against the door of a stall. He needed a shave. He looked sweaty and dusty, as if he had been on the road for a while.

She made a horrible, strangled noise in her throat. *Oh, heavens,* she thought, in panic. Who was this man, and what was he doing here? Warren had been right—she had been a fool to go off alone.

But she hadn't spent most of her life around Fawn for nothing. "Who are you?" she demanded. "What are you doing here? Get out of my barn."

Her voice, she noticed with failing heart, completely lacked authority.

The man stayed where he was. He was very good-looking, she thought irrelevantly. His booted legs were crossed. He had his thumbs hooked under his worn leather belt.

Slowly he lifted his hands in a gesture that said he was both harmless and friendly. "I come in peace," he explained, staring at her with amusement.

She realized she was probably far untidier and dustier than he was. Wisps of hay clung to her socks and her knees were dirty.

He glanced briefly at her legs, then back at her eyes. "I'm from the winery. I have a telephone message for you."

Relief swept over her. She hadn't expected anybody from the winery yet.

"I didn't mean to scare you," he said, his voice slow, lackadaisical, as if he did not so much speak his words as pour them out like sun-warmed honey.

He thrust his fingers into the hip pocket of his jeans and withdrew a neatly folded sheet of paper. On his shirt she noticed a large printed number one. On the chest faded letters announced DuLong Wineries and his name, Rip C. Field.

He held the note out. "You're supposed to call Warren. He said it was very important. You're welcome to use the phone over at the winery."

Embarrassed, Dare shifted the lamp to her other arm and took the paper. She was so rattled by the man's presence that it didn't occur to her to wonder how Warren had tracked her down. She tried to stuff the note into the front pocket of her shorts and nicked her hand on the potato peeler.

"Ouch!" she said.

He shook his head, the corners of his mouth dancing dangerously back toward their lazy smile. "If you don't mind me asking, was the party really that good?"

"What?" she asked, bewildered. He had, she noticed, deep-set gray eyes under straight brown brows. The eyes were pure, unadulterated gray, a startling contrast to his coppery skin.

"What party?" she asked, trying to gather her wits.

"The party in the hayloft," he said, nodding at the ladder. He reached over and took the heavy fire extinguisher from her. "Isn't that when ladies generally put lamp shades on their heads? When they get really uninhibited at parties?"

"Oh!" she exclaimed, remembering the dented lamp shade. She snatched it off and stared at him, too embarrassed to speak.

But he only laughed softly. He hooked the thumb of his free hand next to his low-slung belt buckle. The buckle, she noted with a start, was pewter and molded into the shape of the goat-legged Greek god, Pan, playing on his pipes. Somehow the slightly devilish creature suited the irreverent Mr. Field perfectly.

Her heartbeat slowed a trifle, and she struggled not to smile at how ridiculous she must have looked clambering down the ladder.

But her sense of humor overcame her sense of dignity, and she smiled until she could feel her dimples showing. Her dark eyes met his pale ones for a long intimate moment—a bit too long, she thought.

He studied her intently, still smiling. "Hi, neighbor," his words flowed like warm honey. "Let me carry this thing—" he shifted the fire extinguisher to his other arm

"—to the house for you. You never know when a spark might fly out of nowhere and start something."

Indeed you don't, thought Dare, her mood shifting again. She shouldn't be standing here, blushing and smiling and making such bold eye contact with a stranger.

He was good-looking, all right, with those cloud-gray eyes, his rumpled hair, his high-bridged nose that was kept from being perfect by the slightest irregularity, as if it had once been broken. He might be a vineyard worker, but there was something dangerously disarming in the easy way he carried himself.

She forced her smile to fade into something more seemly.

He noticed the change. "I would have said something to you sooner," he drawled, "but I didn't want to startle you off that ladder. You shouldn't try to get things out of that loft by yourself."

She pushed a strand of her sandy-blond hair back from her face and put her nose up in the air a bit. She had dropped her guard a moment, but she wouldn't do it again.

"I know," she said, trying to sound dignified. "I've called the winery to hire some help."

She started toward the door of the barn. He was right behind her.

"Consider help found," he said. "Me."

He swung the barn door open for her. His arm brushed her shoulder, making her stiffen momentarily.

She stepped outside hurriedly. She should never have exchanged that long, exploratory smile with him in the barn. Yet something within her had responded to the pure maleness of him, and some part of her mind liked his easy insouciance.

"How about it?" he asked, swinging into stride beside her. "Can I have the job?"

"Certainly," she said, unsure about the wisdom of the answer. He was a lot more man than she was used to. "But it's not going to be much fun, Mr. Field."

To her amazement, he threw his head back and laughed.

She looked at him in puzzlement.

"Mr. Field?" he laughed. "Don't be so formal. Call me Rip. Everybody does."

"I think I'll call you Mister anyway," she said primly. His laughter had sounded a little too impudent.

"I think I'll call you Brown Eyes," he said. "Hello, Brown Eyes."

Well, she thought in perplexity, he was certainly fresh, although the sheer good humor in his voice had kept the remark from seeming truly presumptuous. With a pang, she wished that once, just once, Sullivan had troubled to look at her the way this man did, as if she were a young and desirable woman.

CHAPTER TWO

SHE TRIED to take the lamp from him on the porch, but he insisted on carrying it inside. He looked at the small and spindly end table she had brought from the barn in amusement, then set the lamp on it. Then he took the shade from her and screwed it back on.

"I think I liked it better on you," he said, regarding the lamp and then her. He had a rather maddeningly nice mouth, she noticed, a strong, slightly full lower lip, a narrower upper lip that seemed to curl when he smiled.

Stop noticing his mouth, she told herself. She'd been around handsome men most of her life. Some of them, like Sullivan, were too handsome, and that usually meant nothing except colossal conceit.

He turned to face her, hooking his thumbs on each side of the Pan belt buckle again. "What else needs to be done around here?"

She shrugged self-consciously and tried to push the damp strands of her tawny hair back from her face. She suddenly wished she looked nicer. But he was looking at her as if he didn't find her grubby state repulsive, only highly interesting.

He glanced around the room. She had repainted the walls—not very expertly—with some powder pink paint she had found in the barn. She had no curtains on the windows yet.

"I used to come down here and help Freda from time to time with chores. She used to rent this place. She and her little boy. I reckon," he said slowly, "I can do the same for you."

"I'd appreciate it," she answered, hoping she sounded businesslike, but suspecting she didn't. "I'll pay you a fair wage. But some of the furniture is very heavy. Can you handle it alone?"

He raised one eyebrow, his upper lip curling in the barest of smiles. "Honey, I wrestle tractors and heavy equipment all the time. No problem with the furniture. But there's more to do around here than move furniture. If you plan on turning on more than the lights and the radio at the same time, you'll need some rewiring done. The furnace will need work—it always does—the bedrooms are always too cold in winter. And there's one bedroom window that sticks."

She brushed back her hair again and set her small jaw, eyeing him suspiciously. She wasn't about to ask him how he knew so much about the bedroom. Rip Field and Freda must have been very friendly indeed.

He gave her an equally measuring look. "I knew Freda well," he said, as if reading her mind. "She took this place so she'd have time to finish her doctoral dissertation. She was a widow alone with a kid. We're neighborly people in this part of the world. That's all."

Dare looked into his gray eyes, which seemed serious for once. Then she regarded the matted carpet studiously. Neighbors, where she came from, were the people who passed you in the hall and didn't meet your eyes.

Again he was watching her as if he could read her mind. He had a strong, well-boned jaw, and a chin that would have been a bit too long on a less masculine face.

"So where are you from?" he asked finally. "And what do I call you? And when do you want me to show up for work?"

Drat, she thought, stealing another look at his face. He had her off balance again. There was something in those bold eyes that implied instant intimacy, and it sent warning signals ringing through her. What could she possibly have in common with such a man?

"I'm from New York," she answered, allowing herself the slightest of smiles in answer to his. "You can call me Dare. I can use you whenever you have some spare time. Do you work at the winery full-time?"

Rip cocked his head as if work weren't his favorite subject. "Harvest time more than others. Tomorrow's Sunday, and I have the day off. How about then? But right now, why don't you let me get that bed out of the loft for you? You don't have one, do you? Freda had her own. What are you sleeping on? The floor?"

Well, Dare thought uncomfortably, he not only knew a lot about Freda's bedroom, he knew about her bed. She wasn't sure what to think of this man.

"I have a sleeping bag," she replied rather shyly. "There's no hurry."

He set his jaw at a stubborn angle and ran his hand through the springing thickness of his hair. "Sleeping bags are fine outdoors," he observed. "But the floors in this house are harder—and slightly more uneven—than the average mountain. I'll get you a bed. It's the least I can do for some poor refugee from New York."

"There's nothing wrong with New York," Dare said defensively. "I'm not a refugee."

"Then what are you doing here?" he asked, the mockery lighting his eyes.

She had no answer.

"Come on," he said, nodding toward the door. "I'll give you a ride over to the winery, and you can call Warren or whatever his name is. Then I'll come back and get your bed out of the barn."

Her mood went springing off in a new direction. Warren, she remembered, her heart sinking. How had he found her? If he thought he could bully her into going back, he was wrong.

She folded her arms across her limp blouse. "I'm not calling Warren," she said with surprising firmness, in response not only to Warren, but Rip Field himself. He was too much of a take-charge type. Goodness knew she'd had enough of those in her life.

"He said it was an emergency," Rip observed mildly. The phantom smile played at the corner of his mouth again. What did he constantly find so funny?

"Everything's an emergency for Warren," Dare murmured, her dark eyes telling Mr. Field her mind was made up. "I'm not calling him."

"Came here to get away from it all?" he questioned, one brow rising as if he'd heard it all before.

She said nothing, only shrugged slightly. She certainly wasn't going to tell her private business to this stranger, friendly as he was determined to be.

His eyes shone with sardonic amusement. He gave a shrug that parodied her own. "That's why most people turn up in a place like this," he offered. "To get away from it all. Then they find out just how far away from it all it is, and they turn around and go back. But until you do go back, let's get you a bed. You have sheets? A pillow? A blanket?"

Really, she thought, he was a bold one. She wished his conversation didn't run to bedrooms and beds and bed clothes so much.

"Oh, don't look so embarrassed," he jibed. "I'm just asking."

"No," she said, shaking her head. "I can just put my sleeping bag on the bed. I'll buy those things later."

He regarded her a moment, shaking his head in disbelief. "I don't know why you bothered to rent a house," he muttered. "Why didn't you just take a match, a piece of string, your jackknife, and go into the north woods? You could come out once a year to sell your Girl Scout cookies."

"Oh, really," Dare said, not knowing whether to be insulted or to laugh. "Are you going to get me a bed or not?"

He smiled and looked her up and down. He had the expression of a man who was enjoying himself more than he had any right to. "I will get you a bed," he said in his slow, flippant voice, "with the very greatest of pleasure."

As they walked outside she wondered just how he proposed to get the bed out of the loft. She wondered if he were resourceful—or simply cocky.

He wheeled his dusty blue pickup truck to the barn, backed it up and parked it under the open loft door. He took a heavy nylon rope from the pickup's toolbox. Then as Dare watched wide-eyed, he grinned and climbed up the rickety barn ladder as quickly and effortlessly as a cat.

"Now get into the truck," he called from the loft. He flicked a piece of hay down into her hair. "I'll lower the stuff down, but you'll have to guide it some at the end."

She brushed the hay from her hair, listened to his booted footsteps above her, then went to sit on the bed of the pickup. He was awfully sure of himself. He was going to get a surprise when he tried to engage the mattress in combat. If he planned to lower it on a rope, he'd probably be pulled right along after it. She imagined him landing on his overconfident head.

In a moment, he was sitting above her, his long legs hanging out the loft door, boots swinging.

"What are you going to do?" she called up to him. "Try to drop it right on me or something?"

"Tsk, tsk," he said, not even bothering to look at her. "Shame on you, ye of little faith."

"That mattress is heavy," Dare protested, trying to ignore him right back. She picked off a cocklebur that had attacked her knee sock. "If you lower it on that rope, you'll kill yourself and me, too. I don't want a mattress landing on my head."

He was fiddling deftly with the rope and something attached to the loft door. He cast her a look of good-humored contempt.

"I beg your pardon. I've tried to place a few ladies on mattresses in my time, but I've never tried to place a mattress on a lady. A little more trust, please."

Oh, really, thought Dare, darting him a brief dark look, then going back to work on another cocklebur.

"And if you don't trust me," he continued, "you might put some trust in basic physics. Didn't you ever take basic physics? Didn't you ever hear of the pulley?"

She looked up at him again, noticing with a start that the ugly old iron thing on the loft door was a pulley. He was threading the rope through it expertly.

"If you haven't had physics," he went on, tossing her a superior glance, "the principle of the pulley is—"

"I had physics," Dare said, cutting him off. She didn't add she'd got a C minus in it.

"All right," he teased, unimpressed by her spurious protestation of knowledge. "How are you on knots, Girl Scout?"

He had dragged the headboard to the loft door. He was looping the rope around it as symmetrically as if he were tying a package.

"I'm not," Dare said, suddenly feeling inadequate.

"You're not what?" He was hunkered down, his long thigh muscles bulging against the faded denim of his jeans.

"I'm not good on knots," she answered in frustration. "I can tie and untie a tennis shoe. What are you doing up there?"

"Not to worry about the knots," he laughed. "This is a slip knot. Pull one end and it'll come undone. Now be careful. Just guide this onto the truck bed. I'll hold the weight while you do. Then pull the loose end of the rope. It'll be easy."

He braced his heels against the loft floor. She could see the muscles working in his arms as he let the heavy headboard down. It spun and swayed slightly as it descended. She watched his control as he played the rope out hand over hand, exerting more pressure to stop the headboard just before it settled in the truck.

"Get it up against the panel," he said between gritted teeth. "Don't worry. I've got all the weight. Just get it into position."

She eased the dangling headboard against the truck's side. She held her breath, but he was up there, as he promised, holding the weight. Then gently, he let it down. Dare stood in amazement, staring at the first part of her bed, delivered as if by some sun-gilded god of the air.

She tugged the knot hesitantly, and it seemed to dissolve—magic again.

"See?" he said with satisfaction. "It isn't hard to get you bedded at all." He began hauling the rope back up.

By the time he'd lowered the rest of the bed, the springs, the footboard, the slats, and the mattress, the heat of the loft forced him to strip off his shirt. His muscles gleamed in the afternoon light flowing through the loft doors.

In comparison to his job, Dare's seemed easy. She guided seemingly weightless objects into place, while he strained, braced against the harsh pull of the rope.

Sweat was running down his shoulders and chest as he climbed down from the loft as agilely as he'd climbed up.

She noticed, in spite of herself, that he was one of those smooth-chested men with the clean-muscled, hard build of an Olympic swimmer.

His wavy hair was falling over his eyes, and he was flexing his fingers against the lingering burn of rope. He tossed his jersey in the back, helped her into the pickup, got in and drove off, but not toward the house.

Instead he gunned the truck and set off over a wide, mowed path she hadn't noticed before. It led beyond the barn and up through the sumac bushes toward the top of the mountain.

"Where—" she started to ask, but he cut her off.

"I'm hot," he said matter-of-factly. "You're hot. Let's cool off. Then I'll take you back and put this bed together for you."

"Where—" she began again, but the truck jolted as he dodged a rabbit. She was thrown briefly against his hot bare shoulder.

"There's a lake at the winery." He grinned, as if he enjoyed knowing the momentary touch had unsettled her. "Don't worry. It's always deserted this time of day."

"I don't want to go swimming," she said apprehensively. "I—don't have my suit, and you'd better not think I'm going skinny-diving with you, because I'm not."

He gave her a mocking look. "Skinny-dipping, not skinny-diving. And I wouldn't ask you to go skinny-dipping with me. I hardly know you. We can jump in with our clothes on. This is the country. Who's to care?"

"In our clothes?" she protested. "In a lake? Just an old—lake? Without chlorine or anything? It doesn't sound very sanitary to me."

She sniffed in disdain, but she had to admit that water, in any form, sounded nearly irresistible.

"City girl," he said with equal contempt. "God made the lake. And did a fine job of it. Don't criticize."

Before she could think of a comeback, the truck swerved again, knocking her against his shoulder once more. "What was that?" she asked in alarm.

A long-nosed, low-slung animal was trundling into the sumac. It wasn't very large, and it looked like something out of a science fiction movie—a cross between an alligator and a bowling ball.

"Just an old armadillo," he replied languidly. "They come out to amble around this time of day. Perfectly harmless."

"Where do they come out of?" Dare demanded, alarmed. "They don't live in the lake, do they?"

He laughed. "They live in the ground, Girl Scout. And they're moving farther north every year. Who knows? When you move back to New York, you might have one for a neighbor."

"I might not move back to New York," she said musingly. She didn't know what her plans were; she hadn't thought straight since this cheerful but disturbing stranger had surprised her in the barn.

"Oh?" he said, his eyebrows rising in mock dismay. "Disenchanted? At your age? Shame on you."

At my age, she thought, studying his profile. *I've been working since I was four years old. What would you know about disenchantment, you without a care in the world?*

"You might go back," he said quietly. "Most people leave. We've got everything in the world here—except a way to make a living without breaking your back."

His attitude had altered almost imperceptibly. She scrutinized him. The high proud-bridged nose, the strong chin suddenly looked stubborn.

"So why do you stay?" She was curious.

His eyes fastened on hers a moment. "Because I'd rather break my back than leave. Because I love it here. Why are you here? Other than disenchantment."

They had come to a clearing, and the small mountain lake sparkled in the late-afternoon sunlight like a dusky sapphire. On the far side, willows trailed delicate branches in the water. To the north, vineyards swept as far as she could see.

"I asked you a question," he prodded softly, and she could feel his gray eyes on her. "Why are you here? Besides the disenchantment."

The sight of the gemlike lake, the peaceful vineyards, reminded her how complex her life had become, yet how simple it should be.

"Isn't disenchantment enough?" she asked quietly.

"Not around here," he answered, getting out of the truck, then opening the door for her. He stretched out his hand, and she took it, as if it were the most natural act in the world. His hand was hard, alive with strength.

"On top of the mountain we don't allow disenchantment," he said. "Only enchantment, pure and simple."

He looked down at her, and it was a disconcerting sensation. She was tall, five foot ten, and wasn't used to people looking down at her. Sullivan and she were the same height.

"You know," he said, his gaze moving with almost scientific interest between her lips and eyes. "You've got a funny face. A pretty, funny face. It's almost as if you don't know how pretty you are."

Her heart gave an unwarranted little flip, and she felt warm with a heat the August sun hadn't created. She took the smallest step back from him. Somewhere a mockingbird released a liquid bolt of song.

He smiled. "Don't just stand there, Brown Eyes," he scoffed. "Take your shoes off."

"My shoes?" she asked helplessly, unable to take her eyes from his.

"Is that how you swim in New York?" he asked, leaning against the truck and pulling off his boots. "With your shoes on?"

Heavens, he was impossible. She couldn't think straight around him. She leaned against the door of the pickup and took off her shoes and socks. The grass felt warm and spiky between her toes.

He stood barefoot beside her, his belt with the Pan buckle thrown carelessly across the hood of the truck. "Come on," he said, seizing her hand and leading her toward the water.

She followed gingerly, relishing the feel of the grass beneath her feet, which had gone barefoot only on carpets before. She hesitated at the edge of the lake, looking at the sandy mud.

"Are you sure it's all right?" she asked, hedging for time. "Won't the owner object? I mean, this is private property."

He gave her a strange look and pulled her onward. "He won't object. He'd be delighted, I guarantee you."

"Are you sure?" She dug her bare heels in at the mud's edge, imagining the snapping turtles or crabs or savage trout that probably lurked in the lake's depths.

He studied her with sardonic sternness. "I'm positive. And I know what's wrong with you. You're scared. Good grief, to live in New York with ten thousand muggers and then to be scared of clean water."

"I'm not scared," Dare retorted. "And even if the water's clean, the mud isn't."

"Anybody as hot and dirty as we are shouldn't look down on mud," he said firmly. Before she knew what was happening, he scooped her up in his arms and plunged into the lake. She flailed ineffectually against him.

"Ha!" he said, when he was standing chest-deep. Her splashing had wet his hair, and he shook the droplets away vigorously. "Feels good, doesn't it?"

She resisted the natural impulse to put her arms around his neck. The water was cool but not cold, and it felt blissful after her long day in the heat and dust.

"Yes!" she said, confused that she was enjoying his closeness when she knew she shouldn't.

"It feels great," he went on, holding her tighter. "Say it."

"It feels great." She laughed nervously. "But I think you're a crazy person. Let go of me."

"If I let you go, you'll have to stand. If you stand, you'll stand on mud. Just remember, mud feels good."

He released her legs, but kept his hands on her to steady her as her toes searched for the bottom. She felt it and grimaced slightly.

"There," he said, and blew water droplets from her hair. "The bottom feels like warm velvet, doesn't it?"

She wriggled her toes experimentally. He was right. It felt exactly like being barefoot in thick, warm velvet.

"So say it," he said, one arm still around her waist. "Admit you like the feel of it."

"All right. It feels wonderful. It feels glorious!"

He let her go, and she felt peculiarly defenseless and incomplete.

"And that," he said, swimming away, "was only the beginning. Come on. Before we're through, you're going to feel like heaven on earth."

He swam toward the opposite shore with the ease of a man who has swum all his life.

She followed feeling wonderfully cool and carefree. What would Fawn say, she wondered guiltily, if she saw her cavorting around some lake like this? What would Sullivan say? He would scream about what she was doing to his image. Next to Fawn, he was the most critical person she knew.

Sullivan slipped out of her mind like a weightless wisp and blew back to New York where he belonged. But a vague feeling of guilt remained. Rip had already reached the other shore and was sitting under the willows, his body gleaming wet. His faded jeans were dark with water, and his feet were bare and golden on the grass.

Her hazy feeling of guilt was intensified by her realization that she was attracted to Rip Field whom she all too closely identified with the pagan figure on his belt buckle, Pan. Pan the carefree, Pan the changeable, Pan the tireless chaser of nymphs.

Rip ran a hand through his wet hair, wavier from the water. He was watching her.

She swam and played for a while by herself, trying not to be so conscious of him. At last, feeling more controlled, she joined him beneath the willows, her guard carefully raised again. But she needn't have worried. He was stretched out, eyes closed, sunning like a cat. He seemed to have forgotten completely about her.

She sat beside him, wondering why on earth she should care that he wasn't paying any attention to her.

Soon he stretched slowly, and opened his eyes. "It's getting late," he said lazily. "I guess I should make your bed so you can lie in it. Ready?"

She nodded wordlessly. She was suddenly self-conscious of her wet blouse clinging to her small breasts and of her long, nearly bare legs. He was staring at her face, and she felt self-conscious about that, too. She knew her face sent a mixed message to the observer—innocence and experience, virtue and voluptuousness.

He lay on his back, watching her a moment longer. "Come on, funny face," he said at last. "All good things must end."

They swam back to the other shore. The water felt warmer now that the early evening air was beginning to cool.

They took the bumpy mowed path back to the house, and she kept her silence. He had slipped his jersey back on, and it hugged his wet torso. He hummed a tune, his voice low and husky.

"When are you getting a phone?" he asked, glancing at her as he parked in front of the porch.

"Never," she said, with surprising vigor. She had, she reminded herself, come here for privacy, and this man had already disturbingly invaded it. She opened the door before he had a chance to do it for her. "I don't want one."

He cocked a brow and got out of the truck. "A woman alone needs a phone," he said, unlatching the truck's tailgate and heaving the headboard out. "You're a long ways out. Almost isolated. You'll have to have one."

"I'll be fine," she said. She didn't want a phone. Especially now that Warren had found her, it would mean he would be calling her, nagging her, telling her to get back to New York.

"This is a lonely spot, but we get drifters," he cautioned. "Especially around harvest time. And there are some hard-scrabble types around here anyway, as I used to tell Freda. At least she had a phone. And a kid who could go for help in case anything happened. And three dogs."

She tried to help him carry the headboard up the porch stairs, but he shook his head, taking it alone. He carried it, without being told to, into the front bedroom, reminding her how familiar he was with the house—and probably with its former inhabitant, Freda.

"I don't need a phone and I don't need dogs," Dare insisted mildly. "Nobody's bothered me so far. And if they do, I have a gun." She said the last with a certain pride, as if it would show him she knew what she was doing.

He set down the headboard and put one fist on his hip. "You have a gun?" he asked, unbelieving.

"Yes," she said, putting her chin up. She did, too. It was a rather nasty looking black one that Fawn kept in case of prowlers.

"And just what do you know about guns?" he demanded.

"You shoot them," she said with simple logic.

"You shoot them," he repeated sarcastically. "Great. Excuse me while I go carry in a mattress to clear my mind. Is that all you know? Do you also happen to know that you can shoot yourself with one? And not on purpose? That little factor happens to be a major problem in this country."

"Well, I don't carry it around all the time," she replied with false bravado. "I don't twirl it or squint down the barrel. I just have it in case of emergency."

She followed him to the front door and watched as he propped the heavy mattress on his shoulder. He glowered at her as he came back up the stairs.

"Use a gun without knowing how, and you'll have an emergency. With yourself right in the middle. I can guarantee it," he said darkly. "Get rid of it. Throw it in the lake. Throw it in the river. Bury it. And move out of my way."

She didn't like his ordering her about. She'd been very pleased with herself for thinking of bringing the gun. "You know," she remarked, following him to the bedroom, "You're kind of bossy."

"I'm kind of sensible," he replied shortly, then swore as he tried to maneuver the mattress through the bedroom door.

"I'll get you a dog," he said, on his way back outside. "I'll bring one tomorrow. And you get rid of the gun. And get in touch with the phone company. If you want, I'll call them for you."

She stood on the porch, her arms crossed. She tried to put him in his place, as Fawn would have done. "I hired you to get things out of the loft," she said coolly, "not to give me advice on my life-style."

"Oh?" he said, unaffected, taking the springs from the truck. "Don't you know all about life and the universe and everything in it all of a sudden? You're the girl who didn't even know mud feels good." He came up the steps.

"It didn't feel that good," she called after him as he struggled through the bedroom door with the springs. He was altogether too sure of himself.

She heard a thump and he swore again.

"It did, too," he retorted, on his way back to the truck for the footboard and slats. "It felt fine as wine. It felt like honey on a hotcake. You—" his gray eyes shot her a look as he grabbed the footboard "—are very stubborn."

"So are you," she said, leaning against one of the porch posts. Her dark eyes locked with his pale ones. Then, for some irrational reason, she wanted to smile at him.

"Ha," he said, climbing the stairs. "My stubbornness isn't a patch on your stubbornness. And you're changing the subject. Which is your having a gun. A stupid thing for you to have."

"I didn't change the subject," Dare insisted. "You did. You brought up stubbornness. You brought up mud, too. You even brought up hotcakes. You're the one who changed the subject."

She couldn't believe it. She was actually talking back to the man! It gave her a rather heady feeling, a sense of accomplishment.

He came out of the bedroom again, strode to his truck and took a hammer and screwdriver from the toolbox. "Know what else?" he asked, crooking his mouth in disgust. "You argue like a woman, too."

He went past her, and she could hear him banging away in the bedroom. She went inside and stood at the bedroom door. "What am I supposed to argue like?" she asked. "I *am* a woman."

"Yes," he said, giving her another of his ice-gray stares, but there was something humorously ironic in it this time. "I noticed. And a woman alone needs to be careful. When I come tomorrow, I'll bring you a watchdog. I'll bring you a personal appointment with your friendly phone company representative. I'll bring you a baseball bat or a blowgun or a hockey stick or anything you like to drive off intruders. But you give me the gun, all right?"

He was being ridiculous as well as high-handed, Dare thought. Fawn had kept the gun for years, although she never used it. And Rip Field, good-natured as he was, was acting altogether too imperious. Couldn't she go longer than a week without finding somebody who wanted to tell her how to live her life?

"Please," she said, with forced patience, "don't tell me what to do. All my life people have been telling me what to do. If I wasn't tired of it, I would have stayed in New York. I don't need perfect strangers telling me how to run things."

He tightened a screw on the bed. "Don't be irrelevant," he said. He inserted the bed slats expertly. "What's important is that I'm right. I've lived around guns all my life, and even people who know how to use them have accidents. Believe me."

A grimness was creeping into his voice, but she chose to ignore it.

"That's not the point," she insisted, knowing she had to assert herself. "You're trying to browbeat me." She entered the room. "I'm perfectly willing to listen to reason—"

"Then listen to it."

"Mr. Field—"

He thumped the mattress down on the springs as if it weighed nothing, then looked across the bed at her.

"My name isn't Mr. Field," he said. "You might as well know."

She looked at him, her eyes widening. She looked at the name on his shirt—Rip C. Field. In even larger letters on the back it said DuLong Demons, Rip C. Field.

"But—"

"The name's DuLong. Rip DuLong. Or, as you've probably heard the horrible truth, Rupert."

She stared at him in astonishment.

"If you met Oliver McFee, you know all about me. I," he said, half smiling, "am the famed bird poisoner. And so forth."

"But—" she stammered "—your shirt—"

His smile widened at her perplexity. "Rip is my nickname. This is my old softball shirt. I played center field. We tried to have a team at the winery, but harvest always messed up our schedule. We had to give it up. Now—want to shake hands and start over?"

He leaned forward and extended his hand across the empty bed to her.

"Oh..." she said, embarrassed. "Do you really get the mockingbirds drunk?"

"Certainly not. Well—just a little—once. Accidentally. We had a drainage pipe break. It was all McFee needed to go off on a campaign. He loves to raise hell. Are you going to shake my hand or not?"

In embarrassment she put out her hand. "You should have told me."

"I thought it was kind of cute," he said wryly. "Besides, I know Oliver McFee. He probably said plenty about me. I wanted a chance to talk to you without the burden of the abuse McFee always heaps on me."

His hand still held hers firmly. He glanced down at the bed and then at her.

"Why—why does he dislike you so much?" she asked, too conscious of the warmth and strength of his touch.

"For one thing," he said lightly, "when I bought up land around here, I didn't go through him."

"I see," Dare said, wondering how long he intended to keep her hand imprisoned. Self-consciously, she tried to draw away, but he held her fast.

"Well," he shrugged, half-smiling. "I'll be over tomorrow to help you with the rest of the furniture. Sleep tight tonight. In gratitude for all the work I've put into this bed, the least you could do is dream of me."

He let go of her hand, gave her a mock salute and went out to his truck, leaving her speechless.

She'd never met anyone even remotely like him. Ever. He had stirred many foreign emotions in her, but perhaps the strangest was that he made her feel happy. Perhaps it was simply his careless, lighthearted vitality; he had the air of a man born to enjoy life and, above all, a good challenge.

If he'd once accidentally made the mockingbirds drunk—so be it. He made her feel giddy, off center, without the benefit of a drop of wine.

CHAPTER THREE

MORNING BROKE across the mountain with a blaze of silvery light. Dare woke, actually stiff from sleeping on a bed for a change. She stretched and smiled for no reason at all.

Somewhere across the valley church bells rang. Two jays quarreled in the mulberry tree. She rose, showered, and ate a sinfully fattening breakfast—two frosted rolls dripping with jelly fillings and two cups of coffee with cream and sugar.

Barefoot, dressed in white shorts and a white T-shirt embroidered with daisies, she went to the porch and sat in the swing. She sipped at her sugary coffee and stared out over the mountains.

A deep bank of gray clouds filled up the river valley like an enchanted fog. Her long hair fluttered in the breeze that swept from the mountains. She watched a party of quail bob busily from a grove of sumac to the cover of an ivy-draped stump.

New York was 1,700 miles away. Warren was 1,700 miles away. Sullivan was 1,700 miles away. And Rip DuLong was right up the road.

She stretched and smiled again, watching the jays in the mulberry tree. She shouldn't even think about Rip DuLong.

He struck her as a womanizer. Mr. McFee had said as much. Rip could probably no more help paying court than a honeybee could help making honey. But he was treating her as a woman, which was more than Sullivan had ever done. He treated her with a warm and careless ease she'd never encountered before. She both liked it and felt frightened by it.

Dare wasn't the sort to have a mere physical relationship with a man and that was all Rip DuLong would ever want. Fawn had raised her far too carefully for that.

Fawn had taught her that her career was all-important. Nothing else mattered. As long as she was successful in her own right—had a substantial bank account—she couldn't fall on the same hard times that Fawn had. Dare's father had been killed in a coal mining accident when she was a baby, leaving Fawn and Dare with just enough insurance to get them out of that low rent town in Kentucky.

Dare couldn't remember her father at all. Fawn said he was tall and handsome. And she had only vague, fragmented memories of being in Kentucky. Were those few scattered images of remembrance what had drawn her south again? She didn't know. For almost as long as she could remember, it had been her and Fawn—Fawn living for her, Fawn living through her, Fawn living to prove something to the world.

Dare was the American Dream, Fawn had said. Both of them were the American Dream. To rise to such heights after being a coal miner's widow and daughter! To make such money! To be so famous! A classic success story. All because of Fawn's relentless drive.

Sullivan had been Fawn's prize publicity catch. But Sullivan had worked Dare into his schedule as mechanically and dispassionately as he did lifting weights and having his hair touched up. Dare had been confused, then hurt.

"The name of the game is illusion, Sheffy," Fawn would repeat for the thousandth time. "Sullivan's perfect for you. He's what your career needs."

Dare shook her head as she looked into the distance. She was not about to marry a man to help her career. Nor was she going to have her head turned by what Fawn would call "some country boy." Besides, what did she really have in common with a wine-making mountain man with a drawl and a satyr's gleam in his gray eyes? If he affected her, it was because she was getting over Sullivan. That was all.

But at noon, when the dusty blue pickup rolled into her yard, Dare was too entranced by the handsome figure to remember that he shouldn't really affect her at all.

He was dressed for work, in a faded gray western-cut shirt, low-slung jeans, and gray cowboy boots. He had a Stetson tipped back waggishly on his brown waves. This time he was wearing a silver belt buckle, cast to depict in low relief a cluster of grapes.

"Hi," he hailed her, grinning. "I came to move furniture and to boss you about your life-style." His voice was slow and spicy.

"Couldn't you just move furniture?" she asked, willing her heartbeat to slow down.

"Nope," he said. "I've been to church this morning—which I bet is more than you can say. I looked into my heart, and I decided you needed my marvelous advice and aid. So meet Limburger. We'll start there."

He opened the passenger door of the truck and the strangest little dog Dare had ever seen leaped out and began a prancing dance toward her. A pink tongue lolled out of a face that looked like a hairy pincushion.

"What's this thing?" she demanded, staring at the beast, which was now lavishly licking her feet. She did a dance herself, trying to avoid its damp affection.

"That's Limburger," Rip said, as if that explained everything.

"Limburger? A cheese with hair?" Dare protested, crossing her long legs beneath her to protect her feet. Limburger, eager to worship humanity, licked her knee-caps.

"He's your watchdog," Rip said, unsnapping his shirt cuffs and rolling up his sleeves. "I bring you a watchdog and you give me the gun. Remember?"

"Down, down, down!" Dare commanded the dog, but she had to laugh. It was the raggediest little creature she had ever seen. It jumped onto the porch swing, stuck its fuzzy face into hers, and lapped at her chin.

"Ugh!" she cried. "You call this a watchdog? I didn't say I'd give you the gun. Make it behave! Ugh! Yuck!"

"You make him behave," Rip said calmly. "He's your dog. And he's smart. Alert. Protective. Besides, he's a cute stinker, which is why I named him Limburger."

"Limburger," Dare said desperately, "get down! Now!" She set the squirming dog back on the porch. "I don't need a dog," she stated with attempted firmness, but she couldn't help smiling at the funny looking animal.

"Too bad," said Rip, pushing his Stetson farther back. "You've got one. He adores you. He's just like me, poor sucker—smitten at first sight. Now let's go move bureaus and sofas. It's how I always like to spend a Sunday."

"Oh, really," she said in frustration, but she was already in love with the silly dog. Fawn had never allowed her to have pets.

"And," Rip said, standing at the foot of the stairs, "here's the dog food."

He set down a twenty pound bag. "And, here. It's a loan."

He tossed her a neatly wrapped package and she caught it.

"What's this?" she asked suspiciously, peeking into the bundle while trying to dodge Limburger's kisses.

"Sheets and a pillow case. You might as well sleep on sheets tonight. And since this is Sunday, Miss Wicked-City, the stores are closed, and you can't buy any. But if you're going to sleep on sheets, I'd love to have you sleep on mine."

"That's very suggestive of you," she said primly, but found herself smiling again in spite of herself.

"Well," Rip said, studying her as he leaned his crossed arms on the porch railing, "the suggestion was sort of suggestive, but the thought was thoughtful. At least I thought it was a thoughtful thought. Now go put on your shoes, funny face. Make that your boots instead, if you've got any."

"You really are bossy," Dare accused, clutching the bundle of sheets to her chest the way an affronted maiden would.

"Okay." He shrugged, pulling his hat brim down in resignation. "Go waltzing through the weeds with your legs all naked. There are copperheads on this mountain. They have great big fangs, and they love to munch on the ankles of city girls. Don't say I didn't warn you."

The thought of snakes sobered her, and she decided maybe he wasn't so bossy after all.

"Wear some gloves, too," he called after her as she entered the house.

She decided again that he was bossy, undeniably so. His lazy voice pursued her.

"There are brown recluse spiders around here. They like to lurk in old furniture. They have great big fangs, and they love to munch on the wrists of city girls. But don't say I didn't warn you."

Copperheads, she thought irritably. Brown recluse spiders. He was filling her paradise up with all sorts of venomous creatures. She decided to get her boots and gloves from the closet. She shook them out gingerly to make sure a spider hadn't already taken refuge in them.

She clumped back to the porch self-consciously. She had bought the cowboy boots in Nashville, simply because she had never owned a pair but always wanted to. She thought they must look ridiculous with shorts, but Rip didn't seem to notice.

He helped her into the pickup. They drove up the slope to the barn, Limburger chasing happily after.

"I can't have a dog," she said, shaking her head. "what am I going to do with him if I go back to New York?"

He cast her a cool look. "You're not sure you're going back to New York."

"I know," she admitted, twisting her gloves in her lap. "But if I do, what will I do with that dog? He's a country dog. He'd hate the city."

"You're right. I guess you can't go back. It would be dog abuse at its worst. I'd have to take you to court."

"Be serious."

"Why? It's boring. I'm never serious around women."

"Where did you get that creature, anyway?" she asked, twisting her gloves again.

"He's like you," Rip said, parking the truck. "He just strayed here, with that lost-and-love-me look in his eyes.

Like you, he's not much more than a pup. Like you, he needed a place. But I can't keep every stray dog that wanders here. So he's yours. Every farm girl needs a dog.''

Limburger came panting up behind them. When Dare got out of the truck, he threw himself at her feet in submission. She stood watching Rip unlatch the toolbox and take out the rope.

"I'm not a farm girl," she objected. "Not really."

"Aren't you?" He threw the coil of rope over his shoulder. "What else can you be? You live on a farm, don't you?" He walked ahead.

Dare didn't answer. She just clamped her lips together in frustration as she watched his long-legged stride take him into the barn. She reached down and gave Limburger a grudging pat. "I can see you on Fifth Avenue. Rhinestone leash and all. You'd look like a tramp in diamond spats," she whispered.

Limburger only rolled on the grass in ecstasy, trying to kiss her boots. He was in love. He had no shame at all. And Dare, uncomfortable, wondered if she really had lost-and-love-me eyes.

SHE AND RIP SPENT the afternoon levitating furniture from the loft to the truck. It demanded cooperation, and cooperation generated camaraderie. She realized, with a start, that she was enjoying herself very much. And Rip, for all the deceptive laziness of his demeanor, could work harder than any man she'd ever seen.

Limburger lay in the grass, watching it all with an expression on his fuzzy face that told her he probably understood the principle of the pulley better than she did. He did seem like a smart little dog.

Moving the furniture into the house was awkward yet often comical. Rip carried most of the weight, but she had to help him guide the larger pieces. The two of them kept getting askew in their directions, accidentally pinning each other against walls, doors, into corners. She had never laughed so much. Once he made her laugh so hard that she was sure her ribs would break. Drat, she thought, why was he such a likable man as well as a compelling one?

She had become as hot and disheveled as she'd been the day before. Her shorts were streaked with dust, her white T-shirt begrimed. The embroidered yellow daisies looked almost wilted. But when Rip noticed her appearance, he only grinned at her.

His shirt was streaked with perspiration, and he had popped a button off the chest when letting down the heavy dresser. The shirt hung open, halfway to his lean waist.

"Lawsy," he said, when they set the last piece, the purple love seat, into place. He straightened and rubbed his back, arching it. "Don't go back to New York. I don't want to put all this stuff back into the loft."

She pushed her tawny hair back out of her eyes and surveyed the living room proudly. "It looks good, though, doesn't it?"

"Umm." He tilted his Stetson down farther over his eyes as if to shield them from the sight. "Pink walls. Purple couch. Lamp made out of a fire extinguisher. Green easy chair. It'd help if you were color blind."

"Well," she said, nodding to herself in satisfaction. "I like it. It's—it's—" She groped for the right word.

"It's yours," he said, pushing his hat back. She could see his eyes now, amused but gentle. "It's yours because you picked it out, you got it down, you put it together.

And somehow—'' he looked her up and down appreciatively ''—like you, even though all the parts don't look like they should work together, they do. In a strange, striking sort of way.''

She regarded him warily. "Thank you. I think.''

"You're welcome, I know.'' He smiled. "Come on. Let's go to the lake. And let's have some lunch. I'm starved.''

"Oh,'' she said, embarrassed at her lack of hospitality. She really should have provided him with lunch. "I haven't got much. But we can take some peanut butter and crackers and lemonade—''

"Why don't we take the fried chicken I've got in a cooler in the truck?'' he asked, straightening his belt buckle. "And then you can tell me I'm the man who thinks of everything. Even—'' he dug into the back pocket of his jeans ''—this.''

He held out a small piece of hexagon metal. She took it, puzzled.

"What is it?''

"Limburger's rabies tag. I took him over to the vet's last night to get his shots.''

"On Saturday night?'' she asked in disbelief.

"I am not without influence in this county,'' he said with mock pomposity. "I exerted my considerable influence—and the bribe of a case of wine—to keep that mutt safe from virus.''

She was touched, but was afraid to let him know it. For all his flirtatiousness he had been very kind to her, kinder than anyone she could remember.

"I thought you'd have better things to do on a Saturday night,'' she murmured.

"Like what? Chasing women?''

"Frankly, yes." She remembered what Mr. McFee had said about him.

"I've already chased 'em." He shrugged. "None of them could run fast enough to suit me. Now, you've got long enough legs to give a fellow an interesting race."

She tried to keep from smiling, but felt her dimples betraying her again. "You never are serious, are you?" she asked.

He hooked his thumbs beside his belt buckle and met her stare. "About work I am," he said, not smiling. "About everything else—no. Especially pretty girls. Does that scare you? I suppose it does."

The light in his eyes made her skin go prickly. He was always asking her tricky questions, unanswerable questions.

"I don't know why it should make a bit of difference to me," she murmured at last.

"Hmm," was all he said. He smiled.

SHE HAD BROUGHT her bathing suit—a sleek one-piece golden one. She thought she was far too slender to wear a bikini, although she had modeled enough of them. Rip had cutoffs in the truck.

They took turns changing clothes in a grove of willow trees. It was a strange and intimate feeling to stand on the cool earth and slip out of her clothes among the willows, knowing he was waiting for her on the shore.

This time she raced him into the water, and Limburger, who had ridden in the truck bed, followed. He amused himself by swimming in circles and snapping at dragon flies.

Rip dunked Dare, and she, laughing, dunked him back. He dived under the water and tried to grasp her ankles, but she eluded him and held his head down when he tried to surface.

He emerged from the water gasping and growling and shaking the water from his hair. He vowed to drown her. She laughed and told him that if he did, he'd have to move all the furniture back to the loft. He groaned and spared her.

Afterward he took an old quilt from the truck and spread it near the willow grove, then brought over two small coolers. Limburger flopped down in the sun and fell instantly to sleep.

Dare felt clean and deliciously cool. She was also starving. She delighted in the tidy feast Rip spread before them. She realized, with a start, that perhaps she was having the happiest day of her life.

There was fried chicken, crisp and salty, crusty slices of homemade buttered bread, and even a cooled bottle of DuLong Johannesburg. She attacked the food with relish, but she looked on the wine with suspicion.

"What's the matter?" he asked, stretched out on the quilt, leaning on his elbow. He poured himself another glass from the green bottle. "You eat the chicken but you don't drink the wine. What do you think this stuff is—just grape juice with a tendency to delinquency?"

He was still shirtless and barefoot. His brown hair, with gold flecks shooting through it in the afternoon sun, fell over his forehead.

She had donned the white mesh beach jacket she'd brought along so she wouldn't feel quite so bare. She rubbed her flat stomach contentedly and tried to placate him. "I wouldn't know good wine from bad. I've never drunk any. I might go home and put the lamp shade back on my head."

"And a very becoming lamp shade it was," he commented. "At least taste the stuff. It's a nice Riesling, an excellent year—we won awards for it. And the grapes were grown right about there." He pointed toward the nearest section of the vineyard. "So don't let it yearn in vain for your lips. Give it a little satisfaction."

She took a tentative sip and found the wine tasted crisp but elusive. "What am I supposed to say?" She smiled. "Am I supposed to talk like a wine taster now?"

"You're supposed to say it's the best wine in the universe and shower me with compliments."

She took another small sip. "It's not bad," she admitted.

"Not bad," he repeated in disgust, looking at the treetops as if for forbearance. "The woman practically kills me with flattery."

"I told you I didn't know anything about it," she said, laughing. "Tell me what it's like to make wine. Do you really stomp on the grapes in your bare feet and all that sort of thing?"

"Stomping?" He smiled at her. "Winegrowing's an art—but also a science—complete with high tech machinery. The wine making itself I entrust to Ernest. I brought him here from California. I look after the land and the grape growing and the management. Look at this vineyard. Every strain of grape on this mountain is planted precisely where it'll do best. Microclimates, we call them."

He pointed again toward the vineyards stretching away in their green and ordered richness.

"Look at the way this land lies—the way this whole mountain lies, and the valley. It's perfect for grapes. It's been compared to the Rhine Valley land. Look at the soil—" He picked up a handful and crumbled it in his fingers. "It's not your typical Southern soil. It's not Scarlett O'Hara's beloved red earth. It's gray, loose, sandy—not too wet, not too dry—perfect."

His eyes fastened on the vineyards and beyond. He was serious, she realized. He loved this land deeply.

"In the 1800s," he said in his slow voice, "some priests came over here from France to do mission work. Well, Frenchmen are Frenchmen. They knew good wine country when they saw it. They wrote the folks back home. That's how my great-grandfather came here. And this is what he started. With sheer hard work and a gleam in his eye. The old American Dream, eh?"

He smiled sardonically at his own sentiment, but she studied his face thoughtfully. The American Dream. That's what Fawn had believed she had wrested from the rough world for Dare and herself. But this dream, the dream of the DuLong family, seemed far more substantial and satisfying—it seemed real.

She ran her finger meditatively around the rim of her wineglass. "He built all this. Quite an accomplishment."

"We built it," he corrected her, his eyes on her face again. "Generation after generation. We're still building it. At least, I'm trying. Sometimes it's not so easy."

"Why?" she asked. She settled on her elbow, stretching beside him, studying the hard planes of his face.

"Some people stop believing in dreams," he said, spinning the stem of his wineglass between his fingers. "Or their dreams wear them out. This patch of land has worn out plenty. Including my father. I watched it happen, and I watched it break my mother's heart. She wasn't cut out for this kind of life. She should have had better."

He sipped his wine. Dare remembered what Oliver McFee had said about his parents' unhappy marriage. "I'm sorry," she said softly.

He shook his head and shrugged as if he had come to terms with it. "She stopped believing in this place. She shouldn't have. At any rate, I've got two brothers who stopped believing, too. They wanted no part of it. The vineyards weren't doing so well when my father died. The city lights started looking good to them. One's a banker in Atlanta and the other's a plastic surgeon in Beverly Hills. I'm buying them out, and needless to say, they couldn't be happier—but they thought I was a moron when I offered. But it's working. Just like my father knew it would. I've spent the last ten years pouring sweat and money and my heart's blood into this ground."

"And?" she asked. She watched as he set his empty glass on the gray earth.

"And I turned it into wine," he said. "So taste it. Really taste it."

He took her chin between his fingers and leaned toward her. Very slowly, he pressed his mouth to hers. His lips felt hard but smooth. He smelled of the sunshine and the earth and the clear water of the mountain lake. He tasted like wine.

Dare went still. She felt like a sleepwalker who wakens in a place that is foreign and beautiful, but possibly treacherous. He made no other movement to touch her, only held her chin lightly as he kissed her. His lips performed some subtle espionage on hers, softly but surely perusing their secrets.

It was a bold kiss, yet tender. His fingers moved softly to explore the line of her jaw. He traced the curve of her rounded chin, the delicate area just beneath her lower lip. His thumb rested against the pulse of her throat. Lightly his tongue explored the contours of her mouth, then tasted more deeply, more intimately.

For a moment, she felt as if nothing existed except the sunshine and earth and the sweet and private taste of him. The touch of his hand against her face, her throat, felt infinitely right. Her body seemed to beat with the ripening rhythm of the summer day.

Then her muscles tensed, and she suddenly became frightened. She was stunned at how easily she forgot her resolve to resist him. Her own emotions alarmed her, and with something akin to terror, she realized this was precisely what Fawn had warned her against for so many years.

She drew away, staring at him with wide, disapproving eyes. "I'm sorry if you felt you had the right to do that," she said, her voice clipped. "Because you don't."

He raised one brow. His mouth went slightly taut. "Really? It took you some fairly extensive mouth-to-mouth contact before you came to that conclusion."

She flushed. It was true. She hadn't struggled against him. She had practically invited his advance, stretching out beside him like that. She sat up and hugged her knees tightly.

He lay back on the quilt, putting his hands behind his head, staring up at the sky. "It's your own fault," he said, dismissing her. "For having such a damned lush mouth on you. Besides, I fed you and moved your furniture and even gave you a perfectly good dog. You're going to get huffy over giving me one little watery-blooded kiss?"

Watery-blooded? She narrowed her eyes at him exactly the way Fawn used to right before launching a major attack. She wished she had Fawn's gift for invective.

Instead she hugged her knees more tightly. "I'm very grateful for your help with the furniture," she said. Her voice sounded priggish, even to her. "I'm willing to pay for it—by check. I'm grateful for the lunch, but I don't know why I should be grateful for the dog, but if it makes you feel better, thanks for him, too. But I'm not opening the door to—that kind of relationship."

He turned his head and gave her an innocent glance. "Relationship? Brr—sounds somber. Next thing I know, you'll want me to marry you. Too bad. I'm already married. And I can't get a divorce."

"You're married?" Dare asked, feeling shocked and hurt. He certainly hadn't conducted himself like a married man.

He nodded, his mouth crooked ironically. "To the land. And for good. Till death do us part. But I do fool around. Want to fool around with me?"

She narrowed her eyes again and stared down at him. He was looking up at the sky, ignoring her. She was tempted to pour the rest of the wine over his head.

"I don't," she said with some asperity, "fool around."

"Too bad," he sighed. "Because `I'm a confirmed bachelor. The only way some woman will tie me down is if I'm dead. I'm not repeating my father's mistake. Couldn't you change your mind about fooling around?"

She whirled her head around to face him. "You're always joking," she accused, wishing he'd stop teasing her. "Don't you ever stop?"

"No," he said simply. "And frankly, you seem like a girl who needs some laughter. And some plain and simple affection, no strings attached." He turned his face slightly so he could look at her. "So come here and take your medicine. I think you're long overdue."

He reached over, pulling her into his arms. She was so surprised she didn't even have time to protest, though perhaps she didn't want to protest.

This time she gave in with a surge of pleasurable need. He was kissing her so thoroughly she felt as if the wine taste of his lips was slipping into her body, intoxicating her.

He drew back momentarily, leaving her breathless.

"Ha!" he said in triumph, looking at her dazed eyes. "New York, meet Nature." He kissed her again, his bare arms encircling her.

She knew she'd wanted him to kiss her so...she'd known since they'd exchanged that first long and intimate smile. Yes. She had wanted this from the beginning.

CHAPTER FOUR

IT WAS LIMBURGER who broke the enchantment and brought Dare back to earth. He awoke, barked at them happily, then threw himself upon them, trying to lick them both at once.

"Ooooh!" Rip laughed, sitting up and drawing Dare up beside him. "Maybe you were right. A dog isn't such a great idea. Go away, mutt. You don't have to protect her from me."

Dare looked at the wriggling dog. Rip's bare arm draped her shoulder. She felt dazed, even a bit bedazzled.

"I'm not so sure," she said, trying to edge away from Rip.

He held her fast, stroking a tendril of her tawny hair back from her cheek. "You don't do this kind of thing much, do you?" he asked softly. "You're frightened, aren't you?"

"I'm not frightened," she said, turning her face to stare at the lake. But she was. She had never felt such sensations before.

He gently turned her face back toward his. "You are. I can tell. The question is, what are you frightened of? Me? Yourself?"

She shook her head to escape his touch. Her luxuriant hair spilled over her shoulders and she ducked her face, as if she could hide in its shadows.

"Or are you just frightened of everything?" he asked. "You have that air about you. What are you running from, Dare? And what are you trying to find?"

"I—" she began, but could not finish the sentence. She suddenly wanted to go back to the house, to be alone.

"You what?" he probed. "Tell me. Because I have the feeling the answers are important."

"I—I don't want to get involved with anybody," she said. "I can't. It's not even... well, it's the wrong time for that. It's not the time for me to have even a casual... a casual—I don't know what the word for it is," she finished weakly.

She wished it didn't seem so easy just to yield to the strength of his arm and lean back against his bare chest.

"The word you're looking for is affair," he said wryly. He picked up a twig and threw it back on the grass. "You're trying to say you don't want to have a casual affair. The loss, alas, is mine. Is there someone else?"

Someone else, she thought, almost bitterly. She thought of Sullivan, his sleepy blue eyes, long-lashed, the flawless artificial blond of his hair. "Someone else? No." She tried to sound nonchalant.

But she was engaged to Sullivan, or at least she hadn't officially broken the engagement. "Yes," she corrected herself. "Well... not really." Not really seemed closest to the truth. There had never been anything between her and Sullivan—on his side, anyway. She had frequently felt he had found Fawn more attractive.

"Not really," Rip echoed. "I guess not really is a good answer. If he let you walk away from him, he's not really very bright. What else? It's more than that. I can feel it."

She pretended to study the quilt. "I wish you'd let go of me," she whispered.

His arm fell away. "All right. Now what's wrong?"

She pushed her hands through her thick hair. She held them clasped at the back of her neck. Everything would be easier if Rip wasn't so carefree, so kind, so damnably attractive. "It's—it's just complicated," she said. "I'm trying to put things together. To figure them out. And—everything's all tangled up. My mother—"

She stopped, unable to go on.

"Your mother?" he asked gently, putting his finger under her chin, raising her face to his.

"My mother just died," she said. Then, to her humiliation, she began to cry. She had not cried during Fawn's illness nor when she died or afterward. But at last the complex emotions overwhelmed her.

"I'm sorry," he said. He put his arm around her again, and this time she let him. She leaned against his chest and cried so hard it hurt.

He held her until she stopped. "I'm sorry," he repeated. "I didn't know. Go ahead, Dare. Cry all you want. It's all right."

At last she drew back from him, embarrassed, and he let her. He handed her a paper napkin. "Wipe your nose," he said, smiling sympathetically.

She obeyed wordlessly.

"You've been holding those tears in a long time," he said.

She nodded, still feeling shy and ashamed of herself.

"How long?"

"I don't know," she replied. Perhaps since before Fawn's illness? Or maybe she'd been holding them back forever.

"How long ago did she die?" he asked.

She stiffened slightly at the frankness of the question.

"I'm sorry, Dare, but I don't believe in euphemisms—I don't want to say 'since she passed over' or 'went beyond.'"

"I don't either," she said softly. "But I can't help it. She—it's been a few weeks. I knew for months it would happen. But it was still a shock.... So, you see—it's—"

Again words eluded her.

Again he supplied them. "So you don't want to be in somebody's arms for the wrong reasons. Right?"

She bit her lower lip. What he said seemed correct, but only partially so. She agreed anyway. "Right."

"I understand," he assured her. "I wouldn't want you in my arms for the wrong reason myself."

He picked up another twig, twirled it between his fingers, then laughed softly to himself. He threw the twig down. "I hope I'm not lying," he said. "Maybe I am. Maybe I'm just trying to sound noble. That would be disturbing."

She looked at him furtively. "Why?"

He cast her a wry glance. "Because I've never tried to sound noble in my life. I've never much minded why a woman was in my arms as long as she was there. But you—I'd want you there for the right reason. For desire—not comfort, not consolation. I wonder what I should do about it."

"You don't have to do anything," she murmured, staring down at the patchwork quilt again. The conversation was becoming uncomfortable.

"Yes. I do," he contradicted. "You're all dark-eyed and leggy like a lost colt. You've never been here before, and yet you seem to belong here, as if you've come home. You're a mystery. And a very sweet-natured and beautiful one."

She looked up at him. She didn't believe his compliments, but was surprised by his insight about her feeling that she'd come home. How had he known?

"What about this other man?" he asked bluntly.

She stared down again, but blinked in surprise. She realized she had never thought of Sullivan as a man. A beautiful, maddeningly aloof boy, perhaps, but never a man.

She didn't want to answer, but he pursued the question. "How serious is it? Are you going to marry him?"

She shrugged helplessly. "We were—engaged. Kind of."

"Kind of? What sort of engagement is a 'kind of' engagement? Are you still? 'Kind of' engaged, that is?"

His question was embarrassing. She had talked to Sullivan once briefly since Fawn's death. He had called twice, furious at her attitude. Then, petulant, he made vague threats and said he'd talk to her when she came to her senses.

"Kind of," she replied, feeling hypocritical.

"Kind of," he repeated, his teeth together. "You're *kind of kind of* engaged. What sort of indecisive mouse are you tangled up with, anyway? If I ever did get engaged to a woman—God forbid...she'd know it!"

"My mother—" Dare struggled to explain "—arranged it."

"She *what*?" his voice was disbelieving. "What are you, some sort of princess, that people arrange a marriage for you?"

His tone nettled. She looked him in the eye at last. "People did not tell my mother, 'no,'" she said.

"And that includes you?" His mouth had a quizzical smile, but his eyes weren't laughing.

"Especially me," she said.

"You were always a good little girl who did precisely what she was told? No matter what?"

"Maybe I was," she admitted. "Is that so terrible?"

He shook his head as if to clear it, then stood. He put his hands on his hips and stared down at her. "Yes," he said finally. "It is. It sounds like somebody should have told her 'no' once in a while. You, for instance. Then you wouldn't be here in the sticks distracting me while you brood about some wimp who also couldn't say 'no.' How in this day and age could you end up being engaged to a man you didn't love?"

She stared up at him, feeling guilty and foolish. How could she begin to explain? Fawn had been mistress of a thousand emotional weapons to make people do what she wanted. And Dare had once thought she was in love with Sullivan. She was only beginning to realize how naive she had been.

"Who said I didn't love him?" she asked defensively. After all, it had been Sullivan who hadn't cared about her.

"You said you didn't."

His eyes locked with hers. "I never said that," she denied.

"Dare," he said quietly, "not everything is said in words."

Her gaze didn't waver, but her heart began to pound in her throat. She knew what he meant.

"Come on," he said, offering her his hand. "I'll take you home. We can watch the sunset from your porch. And talk—with words or without them. I'm sorry if I made you angry. I didn't mean to speak against your mother. The situation sounds bizarre. It reminds me of an old, old piece of masculine advice."

She ignored his hand and got to her feet by herself. Her knees felt wobbly. "What advice?" she asked, her voice trembling.

He let his hand drop to his side and studied her. Then he smiled. "Very good advice: never eat at a place called Mom's, never play poker with a man named Doc, and never sleep with a woman who has more problems than you do."

She drew in her breath and took a step backward. "Who said I wanted to sleep with you?" she asked, unconsciously clutching her beach coat more tightly to her.

"Oh, you haven't said it—yet," he said easily. He kissed the tip of her nose. "But the time will come. At least, it should come. I think we both know it. Let's not lie. We've known it from the first."

Her mouth fell open and she stared at him with a mixture of rage and incredulity. "Of all the nerve—" she began, but was incapable of completing the sentence.

"Don't worry," he said with a grin, gathering up the quilt in one arm and the picnic remains in the other. "If you get your life straightened out, I may even say yes when you ask. So don't be depressed. Just hang in there. Persevere."

"Of all the nerve in the entire world," she said, stamping her bare foot.

"To want to make love to a creature so stunning her smile practically gives me cardiac arrest? I don't call it nervy. I call it a natural, healthy urge—positively wholesome."

"If you think I would ever ask you to do such a thing—" she began, shaking her head in disbelief.

"But you'll have to ask me." He smiled. "I now see you're too nice a girl for me to make my usual swift and improper advances. Stop glowering. You're also too good-natured to glower."

"I suppose Freda asked you," she said. "My predecessor. You seem to have known her pretty well."

He raised one eyebrow. "You're perceptive," he said coolly. "I'll be honest. No, I didn't make her ask. She was mature enough to know what she was doing. We liked each other. We didn't have anything else in common, but we had that. There was nothing wrong with it. Nobody got hurt."

So, she thought, he had slept with Freda. The knowledge hurt more than it should. Confused and angry, she stalked to the truck. She knew she had been propositioned—and quite cavalierly, too. She didn't know how to deal with it, and she hadn't wanted him to treat her that way. The day was no longer perfect. It was, in fact, ruined.

The man was insufferable. He made her feel things she didn't want to feel. First affection, then desire, then shame. To feel so much so quickly about such a man would be dangerous—far too dangerous for someone as alone and confused as she was.

When they arrived at the house, she politely asked him to leave. His effect on her was too disturbing. Instead he smiled and told her he was changing his clothes. She went into her room and angrily stripped off her bathing suit, threw on safari shorts and a shirt.

She brushed her long hair, and when she came out, Rip was sitting on the porch swing. His long legs were crossed, his boots resting on the railing. Limburger lay on the steps, watching him with worshipful eyes.

Rip patted the seat of the swing. "Come on," he said. "Sit down. We've got lots of talking to do. As John Paul Jones said, 'I have not yet begun to fight.'"

"No," she said, and leaned against a pillar. "I haven't forgiven you for what you said at the lake. And I don't want to fight. I wish you'd go. I want to be alone."

He shrugged negligently. "I won't go home unless you sit by me for a moment. Then I'll go. Fair?"

"No," she said, but she sat down on the swing, as far from him as she could.

He put his hands behind his head and sighed happily. "Wonderful view you've got here. One of the best on the mountain. Terrific place to watch the sunset."

"I'd like to watch the sun set on you," she said irritably. "What you said was totally uncalled for."

"Hogwash," he said comfortably. "I'm honest. I like to state the facts up front. But I'll apologize. I apologize for finding you attractive. For finding you desirable. For suggesting I'd like to rob you of your innocence—especially when it's one of the things I like about you. If it's real, that is."

Dare eyed him suspiciously.

"Ooh," he said, "you must be virtuous indeed. You're still the picture of outraged chastity. I can see this whole thing is going to take some time, so we might as well get the hard stuff out of the way first. Let's talk about your gun."

She put her hand on the chain of the porch swing and stared at him. "No."

He gave her a lazy look. "Yes."

"Don't worry about the gun," she said stonily. "It hasn't been fired for years. Maybe it hasn't ever been fired."

He shrugged again. "Oh, great. It'll probably explode in your hand. Where did you get this trusty weapon, anyway?"

"It was my mother's, not that it's any of your business. She kept it in her nightstand. In case a burglar ever came in."

"Hmm," he mused. "She sounds more formidable all the time. Could she use it?"

"She said she could. I imagine she could."

"What kind of gun is it?"

"Oh, I don't know," she told him shortly. "It's just a gun. Lots of people in the city have them."

"Lots of people in the city accidentally shoot themselves. Lots of people in the country, too. Is it a revolver? An automatic? What?"

"I told you I didn't know."

"Is it loaded?"

"Yes. It was always loaded."

He turned and stared at her. "You mean you didn't even load the thing yourself? You traveled all the way down here with a loaded gun? That probably isn't even registered in your name?"

She turned away from his gaze and watched the sky turning gold and pink. "I was traveling alone. I'd never done that before. It made me feel safe."

"Dare," he said quietly. "I know you think I'm trying to run your life. But the more I hear about this damned gun, the more dangerous it sounds. If you won't get rid of it, at least let me check it out. Let me unload it."

She faced him again. "I won't. And you do sound like you're trying to run my life. Mr. McFee warned me about you. He said you were a—a land baron and a lecher, too."

He put his arm on the back of the swing and stared at her in disbelief. "You're going to believe anything Oliver McFee says? The man would look down his skinny nose at a saint, let alone me—and I'm no saint."

"That's obvious," she said righteously.

He laughed. "You know what I like about you? You try to sound snippy, and you can't. You always sound like an angel forcing herself to scold a chipmunk. I bet you were a nice little girl. And still are. How boring for you."

"It was hardly boring," she said darkly, remembering Fawn's tempers and manipulations.

"And now you've run off to be a cowgirl, with your brand new boots and your trusty gun. I don't blame you. It's even kind of cute. But enough's enough. Give me the gun before you get hurt."

"No."

"You know why you're doing this, don't you?" he asked. "Sheer stubbornness."

"Maybe it's time I got stubborn," she said and crossed her arms. She didn't, she reminded herself, need a would-be seducer with a talent for giving orders, no matter how superficially charming he might be.

"Maybe it's time you learned the difference between somebody controlling you and somebody trying to help you. There is a difference, you know."

"No," she muttered unhappily. "It's all the same thing. 'Do this.' 'Do that.' I'm here alone because I want to be, and I have the gun for protection."

"I think you're here to establish some kind of independence, and you've let this gun become a weird symbol or something. What are you trying to be independent of? What did you do in New York that's got you hiding out here from all humankind?"

"Nothing," she said vaguely. "I—my mother and I were—involved with the fashion industry. I got tired of it. So when she . . . died—" she forced the word out with difficulty "—I came here . . . to make my own decisions. To think things out."

"Fine," he said impatiently. "But be reasonable. You're out here in the middle of nowhere."

"Where I came to live my own life," she said emphatically. What business was it of his, she thought irritably. He was interfering, and he was just one more person who was interested in using her. He'd made it clear at the lake what he wanted from her—friendly sex, no strings attached. She wasn't the sort for that.

"Dare—" he said, an edge in his voice.

"We've talked, and we've accomplished nothing." She rose from the swing and gave him a cool look. "I'm going inside now. Thank you for helping me with the furniture. I'll put a check in the mail for you."

She started to step past him, but he stood and caught her by the arms, staring down into her dark eyes. "Flounce off," he said, scorn in his voice. "But I'll be back. Because, God knows why, I feel responsible for you. Maybe you remind me a little of my mother—naive and kind of helpless. You have no idea what you can run up against out here all by yourself. And guns are dangerous. Keep that—and everything else I've told you in mind."

"I don't," she said, "intend to keep anything about you in mind." She resented his remarks, his insinuations. She might be naive, but she was far from helpless. So why was the touch of his hands so infinitely disturbing, the length of his tall lean body towering over hers so disarming?

"Don't you?" he asked. "See if you'll keep this in mind." He pulled her to him, almost roughly. "Those brown eyes of yours keep saying 'no,' but I think that beautiful mouth wants to learn to say yes—someday."

His mouth bore down on hers with an intensity that shook her heart.

At first his lips felt almost punishing, then their touch changed to something less ferocious, but equally demanding. His hands upon her arms were not cruel, but they were irresistibly strong.

Sensuously, his mouth explored hers. The kiss was as overwhelming as he intended it to be. It was not so much domination as challenge, pure, simple, and electrifying. It was a challenge her own body wanted to answer, and when she tried to gasp in surprise, he only kissed her more intently.

Then he drew back, smiling down at her. He gripped her arms more tightly and kissed her, lightly and swiftly on her full lips.

"Think about that," he taunted, "my little buckaroo."

Then he released her and strode down the steps to his truck. He got in, put on his Stetson, then tipped it to her. "See you tomorrow," he said. He put the hat back on, the brim low over his eyes, backed the truck up and drove down the lane.

She stared after him, half-angry, half-amazed. She'd never met such an audacious and unpredictable man.

"Don't come back," she called.

He only tipped his hat and smiled.

She stayed awake half the night, thinking of the things she should have said to him. He wasn't going to run her life. Nobody was. Those days were gone forever. And he certainly wasn't going to seduce her—casual affair, indeed!

Yet she could not forget the feeling of his mouth upon hers, as if she'd been waiting for his touch all her life.

THE BIRDS HALF AWOKE HER with their chatter the next morning. What brought her to full consciousness was the sound of a truck parking in front of her porch, a door slamming, and a masculine voice singing beneath her window.

Alas, my love,
You do me wrong,
To cast me off discourteously—
For I have loved you so long—
Delighting in your company.

She sat upright, drew the window blind, and stared out in disbelief. Rip stood by the mulberry tree, singing with all his might.

"What are you doing?" she called to him in perplexity, although some secret part of her was glad to see him. "Go away! Are you insane?"

He wore old jeans, old boots, and a fresh work shirt with the DuLong Winery logo. He held a cardboard box beneath one arm.

"'Gone, gone, is the love we knew,'" he continued.

She groaned, threw off the sheet, and stamped to the front porch. She wore a long white nightgown with no sleeves and a high, lacy neckline.

"What are you doing?" she demanded, blinking at the brightness of the sun. She put her hands on her hips. She had on no shoes, and Limburger, who'd followed her onto the porch, thought this meant she wished him to kiss her feet.

"I'm serenading you," Rip explained, "To get back into your good graces. I very much want to be in your good graces."

"Why?" she demanded.

"So we can make up. Go put on some clothes. I'll take you to breakfast."

"I don't want to go to breakfast."

"You said you only had peanut butter and lemonade in the house. You need breakfast. You need fattening up in general. Come on, or I'll start singing again. And I have to admit, it hurts even my ears."

"Don't you ever stop interfering?"

"Since when is an invitation to breakfast interference? 'Oh, Greensleeves was my heart's delight, And, oh, boy, could my Greensleeves fight—'"

"That's not the way the song goes," she scolded. "What are you doing, for heaven's sake?"

"Improvising. Trying to tailor the lyrics a bit for you."

"Well, you can stop right now. I don't know what gets into you."

"Me, neither," he said with a grin. "What do you suppose it is?"

Her hands still on her hips, she studied him, her head cocked. The breeze teased her already sleep-tousled hair, blew her nightgown against her slender legs.

"How do I make you go away?" she asked helplessly.

"By going away with me. Come on. I bet you've never had biscuits and redeye gravy for breakfast. They're wonderful. I came early because I have to go to work. In fact I've been at work since three. It's harvest time, and I'm taking a break. You can't stay angry at me. We're neighbors. Out here neighbors depend on each other. Besides, I brought you a present."

"What kind of present?"

"A survival kit." He grinned, opening the box. "Everything for the city girl roughing it in the country. First, candles and a flashlight. When it storms up here, it doesn't fool around. You'll probably lose your lights."

"Really," she said, shaking her head. He was a rogue, but she was touched by his thoughtfulness.

"Second," he continued, "a portable radio. You'll want it for weather reports if nothing else."

"I—I'm not sure I want a radio," she said hesitantly. Sullivan's voice haunted the airwaves of all the pop stations, and his latest single, "I'll Take Care of Her," symbolized all she was running from.

"You can't live up here like a hermit," he returned. "Around here the weather comes in extremes. You'll need this. Believe me."

He rummaged in the box. "What else have we here? A first-aid kit. A jackknife—great invention. A bird book I thought you might be interested in—and, ah, yes, a nice string of firecrackers."

"Firecrackers?" She tried to keep from laughing. "What on earth for?"

"If you want to scare somebody off, you can light one. It'll sound like a gun. I'm still worried about that damned gun, Dare. I wish you'd give it to me."

"Rip," she said firmly, "I don't want to talk about the gun. Every time we do, we end up arguing."

"Then if you're not going to talk, dress. I've got to introduce you to biscuits and gravy. They taste almost as delicious as you look right now with the wind in your hair."

She ended up going with him, of course. He was right, biscuits and redeye gravy were wonderful.

"What will people think?" she asked, after she had successfully attacked a huge breakfast. She looked nervously around the little café; they were receiving interested glances from curious onlookers. "They won't think—" her voice trailed off.

"That we spent the night together?" he supplied easily, pouring himself another cup of coffee. "No. They won't think that."

"How can you be so sure?" she asked, pouring more cream into her coffee.

"If we spent the night together, we'd be more discreet than to celebrate it with breakfast on the town. Everybody knows I've been up for hours. They also know if a man got a girl like you in his bed, he'd never let her out, even for breakfast."

"Please," she said. "Don't start that again. I really don't know how to deal with it."

"That's what I like about you. You don't know how to deal with it. Fascinating. Truly. I'd think a girl like you would leave a string of broken hearts behind that'd stretch a country mile."

"Hardly," she said.

"Did your mother hold them off with the famous family gun?" he asked wryly.

"Don't be silly," she objected. "There was nobody to hold off."

"I find that hard to believe. I'm holding off one of them for you practically single-handed."

She looked at him in surprise. Warren had tracked her down. Was Sullivan trying to reach her too? The thought was very disturbing.

"What do you mean?"

"I mean Warren, whoever he is, called my place three times yesterday and once last night. How he got my phone number, I don't know, but Tessie—my housekeeper—is tired of taking his messages. So am I, and I only talked to him once."

He reached into his pocket and handed her a creased note. She unfolded it nervously. It read:

Stop this "back to nature" farce. Get to NY immediately. Fawn isn't through with us yet. We got trouble. Call at once.

She looked at the message, then crumpled the paper and thrust it into her purse. "Thanks," she said, fighting to control her emotions so they wouldn't show on her face. "But I'm not calling him."

"Is Warren the fiancé?" Rip asked. His voice was light, but his smile had disappeared.

"No. Warren's a—a family friend. He handled the money for my mother. Kind of."

"Kind of? There's that fateful phrase again. How did he 'kind of' manage your money, if you don't mind me asking."

She didn't answer. Warren was in charge of the money, at least in name, but Fawn was in charge of Warren, heart and soul. Dare supposed there were irregularities in the way the money was managed. She didn't want to think about it. Warren was supposed to work them out. That was his job.

"Not talking, eh?" Rip said, his jaw set. "All right, but Warren is one more good reason for you to get a phone."

She shook her head. "He's one more good reason for me not to get a phone. I don't want to talk to him."

"Neither do I," he told her, his eyes holding hers. "I didn't like the sound of him."

She stared down at her place mat. "I'm sorry you had to talk to him. He can be—brusque."

"Let's not say brusque," he amended. "Let's say rude as hell."

She continued to stare down. She wished she hadn't come here trailing murky clouds from the past. She didn't know whether to believe Warren's message or not, but she knew she didn't want to answer it.

"Dare," Rip said seriously, "this Warren—is he telling the truth? Are you in some kind of trouble?"

"No." She was unsure. "Yes. Maybe. I don't know. I never understood all the ins and outs. But I told him I was leaving for a year. I told him I wouldn't come back before then, no matter what."

"Who's Fawn?" he demanded.

"My mother," she explained, not looking at him.

"What's she got to do with this so-called trouble?" Rip pursued.

"I don't know," she said uneasily. "It's probably just some business thing. The more complicated something was the more my mother enjoyed it. That's all it probably is—a complication. No trouble. Not really."

He watched her for a long moment. "And what if there is?" he asked.

When she didn't reply, he shook his head. "Warren doesn't sound like a man who's fooling, Dare. That's why I showed up this morning. To talk to you. I know you think I'm a meddler, and kind of irresponsible when it comes to women, but if you're really in trouble—well, I'm here. I'll help you if I can. I mean it."

She looked at him in gratitude. His deep-set eyes stirred a yearning response in her. She suddenly wished he was the marrying kind. He had strength in him and kindness, too.

Somebody put a coin in the café jukebox and pushed a button. Dare stiffened. The voice coming from the jukebox was Sullivan's.

The song was his new single, "I'll Take Care of Her." The tabloids claimed he had written it for her. Sullivan sang in his light and fruity voice:

She's a baby, just a baby,
Her eyes say no, but her lips say maybe.
Who is she? A dream? Or somebody real?

Dare's hand began to shake so hard she had to set down her coffee cup. Rip watched her reaction. His jaw tightened.

She wished she could relax under his scrutiny, but she could not. Sullivan's voice filled her with nameless apprehension.

"Honey," Rip finally said. "I just hope you don't have more problems that a sane man would want to handle. And I'm beginning to suspect you do. And that you'd better do something about them—fast. Come on. I'll drive you back to your place."

He knew, she decided. He'd realized who she was. And it appalled him. She didn't blame him. She did have too many problems for anyone to want to be involved with her—especially a man who didn't like involvement in the first place.

She gathered her purse and sunglasses. "I'm sorry you had to deal with Warren," she said as calmly as she could. "But I'm fine. You don't have to keep checking on me. And you don't have to accept any more of Warren's calls."

Sullivan's voice oozed in the background:

She doesn't know her way around.
She's lost and waiting to be found.

Rip stood, threw a scornful look at the jukebox, then tossed a tip beside his plate.

He knew all right, she thought grimly. How stupid of her to have thought that people wouldn't know—to have thought she could live like a normal person.

"You've been—very kind," she said. "But don't trouble yourself about me any longer."

There, she thought. That should give him a graceful exit.

"I'm not in it for kindness," he said shortly. He took her by the arm in a simple gesture of courtesy, but his touch sent a warm current springing through her. "I'm in it for something else."

"What?" She swallowed hard. "What else?"

He shook his head. "Damned if I know. Maybe just for myself. Maybe you're right and I should just leave you alone. I'm starting to think you've got trouble written all over you. More trouble than I have time to deal with. Come on, I'll take you home. I'm a working man." His face looked contemplative, almost brooding.

He drove her home. They hardly spoke.

When she got out of the truck, he gave her a level gaze. "Call Warren," he said without emotion.

She looked at him, her heart beating hard. "No," she said.

He shook his head, his jaw still clamped tight. "I wish I knew what you wanted," he said. "I wonder if you know yourself."

Then he drove away, leaving her standing alone.

CHAPTER FIVE

TROUBLED, Dare drove the winding roads into Arcadia to do some shopping. She needed curtains, bedding of her own, groceries, and a collar for Limburger, who was happily panting in the back seat of the Chevrolet.

The day was glorious, and she tried to enjoy it. But she was deeply disturbed, both by the quicksilver shifts of Rip's attitude and Warren's message.

Warren sounded more alarmist than usual. Any trouble he recognized had to be money trouble, but her money was safe. It had been placed in a trust fund until her twenty-first birthday when she could take charge of it. Fawn might have meddled with it, but she never would have lost it. She was far too canny for that. The last Dare had heard, most of it was invested in a highly profitable company called Saji. Dare knew Sullivan had heavy investments in it as well. But Dare had so little involvement in the administration of her business affairs that the money never seemed real to her.

Although perturbed by Warren's message, she was even more nonplussed by Rip. After breakfast, he had become coolly distant, as if he had withdrawn to some Olympian height where he quietly measured the whole situation and found it absurd.

The situation was absurd, she thought bitterly. He should have doubts about her. If he knew who she was, he'd know she was hardly a real person. No, she was just a creature invented by the press and by Fawn.

She knew the public didn't think much of Fawn's creation, of Sheffy. She was perceived as a glamorous little dimwit, dominated by a scheming mother, but cunning enough to attract a man with a bankroll as large as Sullivan's. She knew that hosts of women thought she didn't even deserve Sullivan, that he was too good for the likes of her.

Yet Sullivan was the only person Fawn had even allowed Dare to date. Fawn liked him because he was as obsessed by money as Fawn was. "Fawny," Sullivan had been fond of saying, "you know more angles than a geometry teacher."

Angles, she thought darkly. Why had the two of them been so fascinated by playing the angles, beating the system? Sometimes she thought she had never really understood them. How could she have thought she loved Sullivan?

In comparison to Rip, everything about Sullivan seemed artificial, from his lightened, carefully blow-dried locks to his beautiful cap-toothed smile.

But Rip, for all his apparent concern, was not a man to become involved, especially with somebody whose life was as complicated as hers. Besides, she counseled herself, if he was kind, he had also seemed far too eager to take advantage of her—or try to. She had come to the mountain to find herself, not to fall under the spell of another dominating personality.

Yet he attracted her on some primitive, helpless level, and it hurt her to think he might no longer want her, even in his uncommitted devil-may-care way, just because of her past—because of what Fawn had tried to make her.

DARE WAS STANDING in line at the supermarket in Arcadia brooding on Rip when she noticed the tabloids by the checkout stand.

"Sullivan to Wed Sheffy at Last!" blared a headline. "See Page Eight!"

She blinked in disbelief. Warren had promised her no more would appear in print about that mythical engagement—what was he thinking of? What was Sullivan thinking of?

She snatched up a copy and put it on top of her groceries. When she got back to the car, she seized the paper and opened it to page eight, hardly conscious that Limburger was kissing the back of her neck.

There were photographs, old ones, of her and Sullivan together. "Rock Star and Super Model Set Date!" exclaimed another headline.

Set date? she thought in disbelief. *What's happening? What are they trying to do?*

Her hands shaking, she read the story:

Sexy rock star Sullivan L. Johns will be tapping his foot to a new song—the wedding march—when he exchanges vows with long-time sweetheart, nineteen-year-old teen-queen model Sheffy.

"We were going to wait until Sheffy was twenty-one," Sullivan said. "But now that her mother, Fawn, has passed on, Sheffy needs someone to take care of her. We were together at her mother's bedside, and it was Fawn's dying wish. We'll be married at the end of the month."

Sheffy's business manager, Warren Kroger, confirmed the news. "These kids have been in love for two years," he said. "It's the most natural thing in the world for them to marry."

Sheffy, the leggy model with the kiss-me lips, has flown to Paris to shop for a trousseau. Although Sullivan was not at the funeral of Sheffy's mother, he laughs at rumors that his absence signaled a split between the engaged pair.

"I had a date to sing at a charity fund-raiser," he explained. "Sheffy told me she didn't want me to let down the audience or the cause. She understands the demands of my career. That's one of the things I love about her."

The twenty-four-year-old rock star declined to say where the wedding will take place, but says it will be at the end of the month.

"I'm an old-fashioned romantic," Sullivan explained. "We want a quiet, old-fashioned, romantic wedding."

A source close to the couple said, "Sheffy is not only getting one of the handsomest men on the rock scene—she's getting one of the richest and the nicest. Sullivan doesn't live life in the fast lane. He's made a fortune from his own recording company as well as his hits. Sheffy was born lucky—she's always been the girl who has everything."

Dare crumpled up the paper and flung it to the floor of the car. She crossed her arms over the steering wheel and laid her hot face against them, her head pounding.

She felt sick. She felt betrayed.

Lies, she thought, *what a rotten tissue of lies.* She was used to seeing lies about herself in print, but these were of a new magnitude. What on earth was Sullivan doing? Why was Warren helping him? Why couldn't they let her alone?

Her head throbbed. After a moment she got out of the car and went to the pay phone outside the grocery. Her hand shaking, she dialed Warren's number. She felt so vulnerable and slightly absurd standing out in the open.

"What is this?" she demanded, when she heard Warren's voice. "I just read a copy of the *World Sun*, and it says I'm going to marry Sullivan. What is this, Warren?"

"It says you're going to marry Sullivan because you're going to marry Sullivan," Warren growled. "Get back to New York. Now. Don't ask any questions. Don't argue, just do it. Do you know what I went through to track you down? I finally traced you through your phone bill to that hick real estate agent, McFee. I told the old crab exactly who you were and demanded to find out where you'd gone."

She cringed. If Oliver McFee knew who she was, soon the entire county would know.

"Warren, I'm not coming back, and I want you to retract this story. You haven't got any right to say such things, and neither does Sullivan. Retract it, or I'll call the press myself. I'll tell them it's a pack of lies from beginning to end."

"You do and you'll regret it to your dying day," Warren threatened. "We're doing what we have to do. This is serious. Stop acting like a child, or you're going to ruin a bunch of lives. Including mine. And Sullivan's. Get back here. You don't know what's at stake."

She took a deep breath, trying to remain calm. "All right—what's at stake?"

"Something too important to tell you over the phone—or put in writing. You should be kissing my feet. Sullivan's, too. That bubble head. But we're trying to take care of you."

"You have an odd way of doing it, Warren," she said, her voice shaky. "I want a retraction, and I want it immediately. No more lies!"

"Do you know what kind of mess that she-wolf, your mother has stirred up?" Warren's voice was edged like a razor. "The woman is actually reaching from beyond the grave to ruin me! I should have known a vampire never really dies."

She was shocked. Warren had never dared to speak against Fawn before.

"Don't you call my mother names, Warren. You always did exactly what she wanted. Don't you dare blame her for anything!"

"I'll call her anything I like, you little fool," Warren raged. "You think you're old enough to face facts? Well, face them. She wasn't content until she had everything. She thought she was smarter than the world, but this time she went too far. She was nothing but—"

He began to swear so foully that she slammed the phone down, then stood staring at it, breathing hard.

She drove home, angry and depressed. She didn't know why Warren had been so enraged. But he had been so beastly, she didn't want to care. Still she wondered, uneasily, just what Fawn had done.

She smiled nervously. Fawn had probably engineered some deal so complex Warren couldn't understand it. But what that had to do with Sullivan, she couldn't imagine. She vowed to stand firm. She wasn't going back. Not yet. And she wasn't going to marry Sullivan—ever. Some day, when life was saner, she would find a man like Rip DuLong. Exactly like Rip DuLong. Except that he would be capable of falling in love.

She tried to forget everything by throwing herself into her housework. Then she sat on the porch swing to watch the sunset, Limburger in her lap. After supper she decided she would try to read. She'd never had much time to read before, and she had brought a stack of books from New York. She hoped she would be able to concentrate.

She was both disturbed and elated when Rip's truck came up the graveled lane. Limburger jumped from the swing, his tail wagging.

But Rip wasn't smiling. He had the same unhappy, preoccupied look he'd worn when he left her that morning. He stepped from the truck, hardly glancing at her. "Can I share your sunset?"

"I guess so," she said uneasily.

He looked as if he had put in a long day's work. He came up the stairs and sat beside her on the swing, crossing his feet on the railing.

He reached into his pocket and handed her a bundle of folded notes. "Your friend, Warren," he explained, his voice terse. "He called the winery every hour on the hour. From noon on. I'm beginning to understand why you don't want a phone."

Troubled, she looked at the messages. They all said the same thing: "Get back immediately. Emergency. Big trouble. Warren."

"Your secretary must hate me," she said, ashamed at having caused so much trouble. She was disturbed by the change in Rip. For the most part he had been lighthearted before, and, in his offhand way, extraordinarily considerate, even if he'd always let her know he was an unredeemed rascal at heart. Now she sensed something darker and more intense in his emotions.

"I told her not to accept any more messages from him," Rip muttered, frowning.

She looked at him with gratitude. "Thanks."

He shook his head impatiently. "It won't do any good, Dare. He'll just have somebody else call."

She gritted her teeth. "I guess I'll have to get a phone."

"I guess you will. I'll call the phone company for you tomorrow. But it'll take them a while to get to you. We're forty miles from the main office." She still felt the restrained anger in his voice. She nodded, feeling helpless.

He put his arm along the back of the swing. She could feel the warmth of his nearness, and it made her skin prickle in the most peculiar way.

"You're a real babe in the woods, do you know that?" he asked gruffly.

She stirred uncomfortably.

"I can take care of myself," she insisted, hoping it was true. The whole point of coming to the mountain had been to take care of herself.

"Oh, you're doing a good job of it," he said, cocking one eyebrow sarcastically. "But you've got a lot to learn. And it looks like you only learn the hard way."

"What do you mean?"

His gray eyes suddenly seemed ominous.

She looked away from him, but she could feel him studying her critically.

"I mean when I brought you that survival kit, I should have put some truth into it. You need it. It seems to be in short supply in your life."

She turned slowly to face him.

He reached into his hip pocket and drew out a folded copy of the latest issue of the *World Sun*. He tossed it unceremoniously into her lap. "That's you, isn't it? The girl on page eight."

Her heart seemed to dry up like a dead leaf. She felt sick to her stomach. He did know. Everything would change now.

"Yes," she said, shrugging guiltily. "That's me."

Suddenly she couldn't bear to look at the tabloid any longer. She tossed it to the floor of the porch like a piece of poisoned refuse.

He picked it up, folded it, tapped it against his open palm. "And?" he asked, looking at her.

"And it's nothing but lies," she said at last. "I don't know what they're doing. But it's lies, all of it. I'm surprised you read such trash."

"I don't read it," he said, his voice dangerously even. "But my housekeeper does. She left it lying open in the kitchen. It took me a moment to recognize the photograph—all that gunk on your face. It didn't make much difference. I realized at breakfast you looked familiar. When you nearly jumped out of your seat when that sloppy song came on, I suspected something. It nearly made me sick. Now this." He hit the paper against his hand again in disgust.

She could think of nothing to say and stared off into the gathering darkness.

"This Warren who they quote as saying you're in Paris, is he the same Warren that's phoning?"

She nodded.

"And Sullivan L. Johns—the lucky fiancé—are you really going to marry him? At the end of the month?"

"No. Not ever," she said softly. "The whole engagement was a publicity stunt. My mother liked him. He liked her. She convinced him that the two of us together would get more publicity than the two of us separately. He went along with it."

"And you did, too?" he said in disbelief. All his muscles seemed to be tensed. "That's pretty cynical for a girl your age."

"Oh, I had a crush on him," she said miserably. "I was only seventeen. My mother never let me date before that. I thought he was wonderful then. I thought someday he'd—oh, never mind what I thought."

"I think he looks like a girl and he sings like a baa-lamb," Rip said sourly. "So what's going on, Dare? How come they're saying you're in Paris? And how come they're saying you're marrying him? In a month?"

She shook her head in bewilderment. "I don't know. I don't understand it. I don't even want to think about it."

He put his hand on her shoulder and shook her lightly. "I think you'd better think about it, sweetheart. You may be a little lady in the middle of a big mess—if you're telling the truth at all."

He gripped her shoulder harder, and she turned her face away from him. "I am telling the truth. I came here to get away from all that," she said. "I don't know what they're doing. I don't care."

He grasped her other shoulder and forced her to face him. "Maybe you'd better start caring. You said Warren's your business manager. Does this have something to do with money? I suppose you have money. A lot of it, in fact."

"I suppose I do," she turned her face away from him. "Does it make any difference?"

"What do you mean, does it make any difference?" he asked, scowling.

She realized that his grip on her shoulders was hard enough to hurt. She wanted to ask, "Does my having money make any difference to you?" but couldn't.

Instead she said, "The money's safe. At least it should be. It's in a trust for me. It's the law for people like me. And it's all invested."

"Oh, Lord," he said, with a groan. "I wasn't after you for your money, if that's what you were thinking. And not because you're famous. If I wanted a woman with money, I'd have looked for her ten years ago, when I needed it. And I most definitely don't want a famous woman. I didn't know I was courting the foremost little sexpot in New York. I don't like to share my women—especially with the whole damned public."

"Oh!" she said in frustration, and blushed furiously. "I'm not a sexpot. And I'm not your woman! How can you even say something like that?"

"Because," he said, his grip on her shoulders tightening even more, "I wanted you to be—before I found out all this. And I never lied to you about the terms. There are no terms—and wouldn't be. It may not be romantic, but it's honest. And I think it's time for you to be honest, Dare."

"I am honest," she protested. "I've always tried to be honest."

"So you honestly got yourself involved in a dishonest engagement. And you sit and let this Johns character escalate the dishonesty. Better get a stepladder, Dare, or the lies will rise up over your head and you'll drown in them."

He stared at her intently for a long moment, then suddenly released her.

He put his hands behind his head, clasping them, leaned back in the swing and looked at her lazily.

"Of course," he said, "maybe you like all the fuss and confusion. Some women do."

"I called Warren," she said, hoping he would understand. "I told him to retract the story."

"Hmm," he said, looking up at an early star. "But you didn't tell him the engagement was off, did you?"

"Well," she hedged, disliking the turn the conversation was taking. "You don't just—do something like that. There are other people involved. Sullivan's career is involved, his image—and all the people around him."

"Oh?" he said acidly. "I suppose you're not involved when he tells the world he's going to marry you. It would be too simple just to tell the truth for once and break this bogus engagement. Unless, of course, you don't really want to break it."

"I *do* want to break it—" she insisted. "If you can break something that doesn't really exist."

"So break it," he drawled.

"What?"

"I said break it. Call the press and tell them the truth—that you're not marrying this Sullivan, and you never were."

She couldn't do that. Couldn't he be more sympathetic? She felt her spine straighten with indignation. One moment he seemed almost disinterested, and the next he was just like Fawn and Warren and Sullivan, telling her what to do. "It's not that easy," she muttered, remembering Warren's warning. "I told you—a lot of people besides me are involved. And it ought to be my decision—not your order."

"You've got a strange way of asserting your independence," he jibed. "Sitting back like a mouse while these people spread lies about you."

"I'm not sitting back," she stated flatly. "You don't know what you're talking about. You don't know anything about that world. You haven't any idea. You couldn't possibly know how complicated it is."

She regretted her words as soon as she said them. They implied her world was more sophisticated, more cosmopolitan than he could understand. His jaw tightened.

"Excuse me. I'm just the guy from the backwoods," he said, standing up.

He hooked his thumbs on each side of his belt buckle. "But, bumpkin that I am, I know a thing or two. One, I don't like lies—for any reason. Two, if you've got a problem with this Warren, you'd better solve it, not try to ignore it until it goes away. For your own good."

"Why are people always telling me what to do for my own good?" she demanded.

"Maybe you need to be told," he replied coolly.

"So everybody seems to think," she said bitterly.

"Or is this just a part of a publicity stunt?" he asked, staring down at her. "Sheffy mysteriously disappears. Maybe that'll be next week's headline. I suppose that sort of thing is always good for instant publicity."

"I hate the headlines," she said, looking up at him, tears filling her eyes. "I hated my life back there. It was a circus, a stage show, nothing but phoniness."

"Or maybe," he drawled, "you're more like your mother than you think. Maybe you've got Warren and this Sullivan right where you want them—begging for you to come home. And your return to nature thing is a very bright power play on your part. And you can amuse yourself with the country boys until the city boys do exactly what you want. Is that it?"

She stood up and faced him, glad the evening's shadows hid the pain in her face.

"That's cruel," she accused, struggling to keep her voice steady. "Maybe you should write for those papers. Your imagination is ugly enough. And don't criticize my mother. You didn't even know her. Everybody criticized her, but she did what she had to do. We came to New York practically without a dime to our names—"

"And—" he cut her off "—you left with lots of dimes, but no name to call your own—*Sheffy*," he said contemptuously.

"It was a professional name," she said in her own defense. "There was already a Dareen Clark modeling, and a Marla Dare. Sheffy was a silly name and I hated it, but I had to have one that stood out. It doesn't have anything to do with all this."

"Sorry," he said tersely. "But it seems to have a lot to do with all this. You say you came here to get away from it all. So I'd like to believe. But if you really want to get away, you've got a funny way of showing it."

"What's that supposed to mean?" she asked in frustration.

"It means if you don't want their phony world, then don't play their phony games. And don't play games with me."

"I'm not playing games with you," she protested, turning and gripping the porch railing. She blinked hard, looking off into the distance.

He stepped up behind her, so close she could feel the heat of his tall body. "You didn't tell me who you really were."

"You didn't ask." She gripped the railing more tightly. "And I didn't think it mattered. I wanted to be treated like an ordinary person."

"You act like the most natural, unaffected girl in the world," he said between his teeth. "You act like you belong here. But maybe you're just a spoiled kid—how do I know? You say you want to take care of yourself, but then you sit back and let people manipulate your life from a thousand miles away. Maybe you've got to the point where you like being used—and using."

She leaned her forehead against a pillar. The wood felt rough, uncomforting. "You didn't tell me who you were at first, either," she defended herself. "You said you wanted to be taken for what you were. Why couldn't I do the same thing?"

"The situations don't even compare," he said, his voice tight. "I didn't know you were a big-time celebrity with a past as complicated as a Chinese puzzle."

"What do you care?" she asked miserably. "It's not as if I matter to you. You don't want to get involved. You said so yourself."

He grasped her by the arms and turned her toward him. "I never said you didn't matter to me."

She looked up at him, her heart thudding swiftly.

"I said I wasn't the marrying kind—unlike your pretty blond friend. You've seen the hours I put in. I'll be putting them in for years. It's not the kind of life I'd ask a woman to share. It may not be the kind of life a woman can share."

"So you'd just like to share your advice and your bed," she retorted bitterly.

"What's wrong with that?" he challenged. "The advice is sound and the bed is warm. Things could be good between us. There's a basic attraction between us. There has been from the start. Before we even really knew who the other was. Don't deny it."

She looked up at him. Even in the failing light she could feel the intensity of his gaze, locking with hers for a long moment. She felt something deep within her take a skip, a flutter, then die.

He seemed to know what his touch did to her. He nodded, as if in satisfaction. "Do you want what's real?" he asked. "Or are you just pretending?"

Her heart pounded against her chest so hard she could hardly breathe.

"What's real," he whispered, "isn't always what's safe." His touch on her shoulders grew harder. "Sometimes it means taking chances. With no guarantees. No promises made. Just chances. Like this."

He bent his face to hers and kissed her, a long, ardent kiss.

The taste of him, the touch of him, the heady, masculine scent of him, made her senses well up in celebration. When his tongue probed softly at her lips, she parted them, inviting the greater intimacy.

Boldly his mouth explored hers, and her own lips more shyly ventured against his.

She felt one of his hands gather the wealth of her hair into a silken handful at her nape, while the fingers of the other undid the top buttons of her blouse.

The warmth of his hand closed lightly over one breast, caressing, and she felt herself leaning more closely to him, to savor and intensify his touch.

His mouth moved to the hollow of her throat, then she felt it, hot, moist, and demanding, pressed between her breasts as she bent back helplessly, wanting more of this, more of him.

Then a jolt of coldness shot through her as she realized what she was doing. Her body stiffened, and she thrust him away, pulling her blouse shut.

He stood staring at her, smiling with a slightly mocking crook to his mouth. "Ah," he breathed. "Things got a bit too real, did they? I thought so. Relax, love. If you want the whole, fascinating, dangerous tour of reality, we'll do it the right way—slowly. But you'll have to know your own mind. And you'll have to be a free woman. You'll have to be really in charge of your own life."

Expertly, he moved her hand aside and refastened a button. "I love blouse buttons," he said flippantly. "I think of them as keys that unlock a treasure chest, if you'll excuse the pun."

"I—" she stammered. "I—"

"You," he said, tilting her chin up to his gaze, "are a woman who wants to make choices. Well you'd better start making them. I'm a busy man. I don't know how long I want to wait around for you to grow up. You want real life? This is it. It comes with no warranties."

He stepped back and put his hands in his hip pockets, then strolled down the stairs with elaborate casualness. "See you around, neighbor," he said over his shoulder.

He climbed into the truck and started the engine. "When you're brave enough to take chances—let me know. Assuming, of course, you're not—how shall we say?—otherwise engaged."

She watched him drive down the lane, the lights disappearing into the darkness.

She stared after him, her heart still pounding. He was still angry and his words had hurt. Instinctively she put her hand to her chest, as if she could press the pain away.

Had he believed anything she said? She wasn't even sure.

But he had kissed her. That showed he still cared, didn't it? No, she thought—it proved nothing. He merely wanted her...with no promises, no commitments, for his own pleasure.

CHAPTER SIX

THE NEXT DAY Dare's mood darkened further when she found the letter. She had been cleaning behind the baseboard heater when she discovered a mysterious envelope. It was sealed, and bore neither address nor stamp. Curious, she opened it. It contained two neatly typed pages and the flourishing signature, "Freda." After Freda wrote it she must have sealed it, then lost it somehow. Dare knew she shouldn't read it. It was wrong. But she couldn't resist. Then she wished she had not read it at all.

Dear Sis—

Sorry to be so long between letters, but I'm busy polishing the dissertation—almost done—hurray! Timmy's loved this stay in the country, and it's done him worlds of good, but I'm ready for city life again—I miss bright lights, crowds, and HUGE shopping malls! This is a great place to work, but I could never live here. There's such a thing as too much scenery!

No, no, no, this "new man" is not to be mentioned to Mom—under any circumstances. There's nothing serious between us. But sometimes I look at him and wonder, how did I get so lucky? Rip Du-Long is something, Tina, a man who has it all: honesty, looks, drive, intelligence, humor, kindness you wouldn't believe. Did I leave out muscles? Like I said he's got it all!

What he doesn't have (and I don't either at this point) is any interest in long-term commitments. He's very up-front about it—he's up-front about everything—his parents' marriage has made him wary, and his drive is concentrated with almost frightening single-mindedness on building up his winery. He believes in affection, but not in falling in love. But heavens, he's been wonderful to me, and Timmy, too.

If I'm honest with myself, I know I'm still not over Robert's death, and I know Timmy isn't. For two years I've thrown myself into work, and now, thanks to Rip, I think I'm learning to live again. We take our relationship one day at a time. He's been good for me, Tina, so good. But Mom, I repeat, would NEVER understand or forgive this casual, happy thing between us. You will, and I love you for it.

Love and kisses,
Freda

Dare felt tears of jealousy and unhappiness sting her eyes. She envied the intimacy Freda must have shared with Rip, and she envied the older woman's maturity— her willingness to take things as they were. The words of praise for Rip hurt. Freda was right. He had all those things—honesty, intelligence, drive, kindness. But he was not the marrying kind. Freda accepted it, philosophically, even blithely. But Dare could not, and it made her feel young, foolish, and more insecure than ever.

What she learned from Freda's letter didn't make her encounters with Rip become any easier. Each day, he checked on her twice. He came in the morning, taking a break from the rigors of harvest, to see if she was all right or needed anything. He came after work as well, usually around sunset. He was neighborly. He was kind in his teasing way. He seemed concerned. But he no longer made any move to touch her, to take her in his arms. She wondered if he were no longer interested, now that he knew who she was.

Their conversations were always strained. He'd ask if she had dealt with Warren's emergency. She'd reply that Warren could work out his own emergency.

He'd ask if she was still engaged. She'd reply that she had never been engaged, not really. Then they would look at each other until Dare, feeling guilty, looked away.

On Thursday, he'd infuriated her by singing Sullivan's hit song in his off-key bass to himself:

> She doesn't know her way around.
> She's lost and waiting to be found—

"I wish you wouldn't sing that," she asserted, doing her best to glare at him. "I happen to hate that song."

"Really?" he asked, cocking an eyebrow innocently. "I like it. It speaks volumes. The guy's a genius. He's got your number. Maybe you should marry him. I think you're the marrying kind. That's why you're so afraid of me."

"Will you change the subject?" she asked, feeling the familiar surge of anger and hurt.

"Okay," he said easily. "Been listening to your radio? Looks like we're in for some big storms this weekend."

"No. I hate the radio. I'm cleaning the cellar and I'm straightening the barn, and it's a full-time job giving

Limburger baths. Every time he steps outside, a dozen fleas jump on him."

"You're spoiling him. I didn't mean him to be a house pet. A few fleas never hurt a dog."

She tried to ignore him, but he stared at her, his lip curling. "I don't know why, for God's sake, you're worried about fleas," he went on. "You've got bigger problems. Or are you really going to sit here and wait for all your troubles to disappear? You think if you hide long enough—poof!—they'll vanish?"

"Is this the end of the sermon?" she asked impatiently.

"Yes. For now."

Their eyes locked and Dare could feel a subtle and odd change in mood. The tension didn't go away, but there was more than tension between them now—something that bound them together in spite of themselves, as if they shared some mysterious secret that could be neither communicated nor forgotten. Disturbed, Dare remembered what he had said about the immediate and primal attraction between them.

He got back in the truck. "Better put your life in shape, kid," he said, leaning out the window, that smug look on his face.

The word *kid* hurt. "You're bossy," she said. "You're maddening."

"You like it." He grinned. "I have the feeling you've been waiting for years for somebody to come along and madden you. In the right way, of course."

Then he'd driven off, leaving her feeling lonely and confused, wondering if he was right about Warren and Sullivan. She knew he would make no move toward her until she had dealt with Sullivan. And then he would simply bring up the matter of a meaningless affair again.

The thought frightened her, made her even more reluctant to take any decisive action.

She hoped Warren had heeded her warning and retracted the marriage story. That, at least, would give her time to think, to sort out her feelings.

Warren was resorting to telegrams now, at least two a day. After the first three, she refused to read them. She tossed them unopened into the trash. The message was the same each time: "Get back to the Big Apple before I come and drag you back. Sullivan's sick of this escapade and so am I. Get back or be prepared to sit on that mountain forever."

The only advantage was that she was getting to know the Western Union man who delivered the telegrams. His name was Billy Bob Fribble, and he was as thin, laconic, and good-natured as an old hound dog.

"You seem awful popular," he drawled when he delivered the fifth telegram.

"Not popular," she said, signing for it. "In fact, just the opposite." She gave him a tired smile.

"You're that model-lady, ain't you?" he asked, tipping his cap back on his thinning brown hair. "Word's out, you know. Some people has recognized you. I hope you don't mind me amentionin' it."

Her smile was strained. She shook her head. Trust Oliver McFee to spread the good word, she thought.

"You ain't the first celebrity we had down here," Billy Bob said with a trace of pride. "We had a writer once— a poet-feller. And a United States Supreme Court judge comes down here ever winter for the duck huntin'. And a catcher for the *De*troit Tigers baseball team retired here. But we reckon folks like you come down for your privacy, so we try not to bother none. Basically folks is folks."

"People have been very kind, very friendly," she said gratefully.

"And you got yourself a nice neighbor," Billy Bob continued. "Old Rip, he's as good a neighbor as you could ask for. Some talks against him, sayin' he bought out all the other grape growers to make hisself a fortune. And he'll make hisself a fortune, too. Smart feller. But he saved them other farmers and winegrowers from theirselves, and most folks know it. A bunch a little wineries, now they just ain't gonna make nothing. One big one, it can, and it will, 'cause he's worked pure wonder with it."

"He seems to have done very well," she replied, beginning to feel uncomfortable at hearing Rip's praises sung.

"Now there was some that said that boy didn't have a serious bone in his body," Billy Bob observed, nodding wisely. "And when he was younger, he was a hellion and a scamp, no doubt about it. But when his daddy died, and the chips was down, it was ol' Rip saved the winery. He showed folks what he was made of then. Best of all three of the DuLong boys, if you ask me."

"I'm sure he's—uh—very admirable."

"Yep. Though some'll say otherwise. I just thought I'd put my two cents in. Some fault him because he's not the marryin' kind. Well, I don't. Ain't the marryin' kind myself. There's some of us men what's born to be free. Nothin' wrong with that."

He tipped his cap, got back in his van and drove off. Dare smiled in spite of herself and shook her head. Trust men to stick together, she thought.

RIP AND BILLY BOB were not her only callers that week. On Friday, the realtor, Oliver McFee, pulled up in her front yard. He was driving an ancient black Dodge, and a woman who looked as thin and sour as he did sat beside him in the front seat.

Mr. McFee got out of the car, nodded curtly to Dare, then walked around to the passenger side to open the door for the older woman. She stepped out as if she were empress of the county.

"This is Mrs. Bailey," Mr. McFee said in his reedy voice. "The owner. We thought we would take a spin and see how you were keeping up the property."

Mrs. Bailey was taller than Mr. McFee, and she was dressed in an old, unfashionable dress with a faded print. Her feet were shod in sensible black shoes, and she had a small, faded, black hat skewered to her iron-gray hair with what seemed to be a hundred hairpins. But the pearls she wore in a rope around her corded neck looked real, and she carried a walking stick whose head glittered as only real gold can.

Limburger began to bark at the two furiously from the top of the porch stairs. Dare scooped him up and shushed him.

Mrs. Bailey glowered at the dog through her trifocals. "I hope," she said nastily, "that you do not let that dog in my house. Dogs shed their filthy hair on carpets, and I put that carpet in only twelve years ago."

"He's very clean," Dare replied nervously.

"That carpet was almost as good as new when I put it in." Mrs. Bailey sniffed. "I had it in my very own dining room for ten years, and it's of the finest quality. I don't want some mongrel destroying it."

"I wasn't aware she'd acquired a house dog," Mr. McFee said, assisting Mrs. Bailey creakily up the stairs. He shot Dare a dangerous look. "Perhaps we shall have to ask you to put down a pet deposit, Miss Sheffield. As insurance against damage. Either that, or have you get rid of the dog."

"I'll be glad to put down a deposit," she said hastily, hugging Limburger more tightly.

"Seventy-five dollars should be sufficient," Mr. McFee said, fastening a malevolent gaze on Limburger.

"Eighty-five would be even more sufficient," croaked Mrs. Bailey, eyeing the dog with even greater distaste.

"We'll just step inside," said Mr. McFee, opening the screen door for Mrs. Bailey, "to see how things look."

The two entered, and Dare, piqued, followed them, Limburger still in her arms.

"She has painted the walls." Mrs. Bailey sniffed. "That paint looks suspiciously familiar. It came out of my barn, I know. It was given to me by my nephew Elmo. I was saving it."

"Have you used Mrs. Bailey's paint without permission?" asked Mr. McFee, aghast.

"You said I was welcome to use anything I found in the barn," Dare explained. "The walls needed painting."

"Put down another twenty-five dollars for paint," Mrs. Bailey said curtly. "I will not have my own tenant pilfering my paint. And I do believe she's scratched my love seat. Yes. It is marred, no question."

Dare squinted at the freshly polished love seat. It seemed no more scratched to her than when she found it in the barn. "I think it was scratched already," Dare said quietly.

The old woman shot her a haughty look.

Carefully and relentlessly Mr. McFee and Mrs. Bailey toured the house. Mrs. Bailey even opened the medicine cabinet and peered in the kitchen cupboards.

"You are far neater than I expected," she said, after getting down on her creaking knees and examining the cabinets beneath the sink. "I highly doubted one in your—position—would be tidy."

"I beg your pardon?" Dare said, watching Mr. McFee assist Mrs. Bailey to her feet. "What do you mean—one in my position?"

"Oof," said Mrs. Bailey, ignoring her. "To the bedroom, Oliver."

The two had already glanced in the back bedroom and now headed inexorably toward the front one where she slept.

"Hmmm, only one pillow," reflected Mrs. Bailey, poking it soundly. "Of course, that may mean nothing at all." She turned and peered into the closet. "Only women's clothes," she muttered, disappointment in her voice. "Of course, these days it's so difficult to tell." She glanced at Dare's long legs and shorts contemptuously. "In my day," she asserted, "the only women who wore trousers were those who worked in rivet factories or something. It was a lower class phenomenon."

"I rather think it still is." Mr. McFee nodded piously.

"Have you seen enough to suit you?" Dare asked, her patience at an end.

"Very nearly," answered Mrs. Bailey, leaning on her gold-headed stick. "I wanted to make certain you were living alone."

"Living alone?" Dare asked in disbelief. "Of course I'm living alone."

Mrs. Bailey inspected the bed again, as if she might have missed the telltale imprint of a male body. "And I wished to see you," she said shortly, her eyes meeting Dare's again. "Neither Mr. McFee nor I realized I was renting to someone infamous."

Dare's heart sank at exactly the same rate her anger rose. "Oh, really," she said, disgusted.

"I did not realize my house was being rented to some-one who had posed in the—dare I speak the word?—the altogether."

"I've never posed nude in my life," Dare said be-tween gritted teeth. She may have posed in a bikini, but never in the nude. "I never did and I never will."

"Your mother should have been horsewhipped," Mrs. Bailey said shortly. "I've read about her. No daughter of mine would have been so exploited."

Dare took a deep breath. "When my mother started out she didn't own any rental property, Mrs. Bailey," she said grimly. "Or any pearls or a gold-headed cane. She didn't have anything in the world except a child to take care of—and her wits. I don't like hearing her criti-cized."

"Umph," grunted Mrs. Bailey. "Perhaps you have a bit of spunk after all. I had expected no better than a puppet and a poppet. You can imagine my hesitation to continue renting to so feckless a young thing."

Dare took another deep breath and briefly considered setting Limburger on the floor. She would point her fin-ger at Mrs. Bailey and Mr. McFee and give the com-mand "Kill!" Limburger wouldn't know what she meant, but it would give her momentary satisfaction.

"Ha!" laughed Mrs. Bailey unpleasantly. "Rumor, rumor, rumor—it's everywhere. Small towns. Big towns. The whole world is a mill of rumor. That's why I came to see you for myself. Yes, I wanted to see you."

So, Dare thought. That was why she was here—to peer at the freak. That, and to try to squeeze some more money out of the house. "Well," she replied, willing control into her voice, "I hope your glimpse has been satisfactory. I really don't have any more time for this. I don't recall my lease saying I was subject to routine inspections. So, if you don't mind—"

"My glimpse has been a glimpse, that's all," Mrs. Bailey snapped. "And business is business, that's all. Do you intend to marry this—this singer person? Do you intend to break your lease?"

"No," Dare said rather hotly. "I do not intend to break the lease. I've paid my rent in advance, and I'm not leaving, if that's what you're worried about. And I'm not getting married, so nobody's moving in with me, either. I suppose you'd want more rent if another person lived here. Well, there's me and there's Limburger, and that's it."

"Oh, don't be bumptious," Mrs. Bailey said imperiously. "This is my property. I have a right to know who I'm renting to and what's going on."

"Indeed she does," affirmed Mr. McFee, examining the perfume bottles on Dare's dresser. "She has a perfect right."

"I rented out this house as a domicile, not a refuge," Mrs. Bailey continued, with pleased malice. "I don't know what you're doing here, and I am not altogether sure I approve."

"I'm not doing anything. I came here to be alone."

"Alone?" Mrs. Bailey laughed bitterly. "Life will bring you enough of that!"

She looked at Dare's bare hands with interest. "The young person to whom the papers say you are engaged," said Mrs. Bailey, "does not look quite right to me. He does not appear wholesome. For instance, he wears a ring in his ear. I should question the normalcy of any man who wore a ring in his ear."

Dare sighed. There was no way she was going to try to explain Sullivan's silly earring. He wore it because a hundred other rock singers wore them; it was almost like a part of a uniform.

"Yet, you say you're not going to marry the creature. Hmmph. I must admit, you do surprise me. Not at all what I expected. If I didn't know who you were, I'd take you for an ordinary person. Yet—if you're not going to marry this boy, why do the papers say so? I suppose it comes down to money, doesn't it? It most generally does."

A tiny shaft of logic pierced Dare's anger. This was something Mrs. Bailey and Mr. McFee would understand. "Yes," she replied, hoping to end the conversation. "They say it's because of money. Good or bad, publicity is money. And that's all there is to it."

"Love and money. Money and love," mused Mrs. Bailey. She stroked her pearls and looked at Dare with a strange, almost hungry expression. "Money and love and rumor. Around it goes and around it goes."

Some strange thoughts were spinning away under Mrs. Bailey's pinned and faded hat. Her thin lips smiled a cynical smile. Her pale eyes gleamed.

"And Mr. DuLong," she continued, her eyes still fastened on Dare's. "Mr. DuLong has been—neighborly, I take it."

"Neighborly enough," Dare said, rather brusquely.

Mrs. Bailey smiled. "He's finally made that winery a success, hasn't he? Against all the odds and after all this time, one of them has finally made it a success."

"He seems to have done well enough," Dare replied noncommittally.

"Who would have thought it?" Mrs. Bailey said, knotting her fingers around the head of the cane. She stared through the sheer bedroom curtains at the mulberry tree in the front yard. "Who would ever have taken that boy seriously? Yet of all them, he's most like his grandfather. When that old man was young, you wouldn't have thought he cared for anything but laughter—and wooing. Then the hard times came, but he hung on to his fool land. There were as many rumors about him as about this young one, this Rip...more. Well, they do care for their precious land . . . but that's all."

Dare watched her, confused. The old woman seemed to have slipped into the past.

Mr. McFee sensed it, too. "Tabitha," he said gruffly. "Mrs. Bailey. I must get back to the office. Do you—"

Mrs. Bailey cut him off with a wave of her gnarled hand. "Do I want to raise the rent, Oliver? No. No, I don't—"

Mr. McFee's thin face reddened, and he cast Dare a guilty and disapproving glance. "But you said—"

"I said I would look over the situation and see if a raise was in order. No."

She gave Dare a long appraising look. "Have her write you a check for the pet deposit and the paint. That is all."

"What about the scratch on the love seat?" Mr. McFee prodded. "That's a very fine piece, that love seat."

"Pah!" exclaimed Mrs. Bailey. "It's a horror and it's always been scratched. No."

"But—" he began, glancing nervously at Dare again.

Mrs. Bailey tapped the pillow with her cane, as if to bring Mr. McFee to an appropriate degree of discipline. "Push her no further, Oliver. Nor me. She is not what I expected. Even though I understand gossip better than most. I want her in this house. The rent remains the same."

Mr. McFee looked sulky, and Dare's mouth opened in surprise.

"Why?" she asked. "Why do you want me here?"

Mrs. Bailey looked out the window again. She stroked her pearls as if they were a pet snake coiled around her neck. "To see what happens this time," she said hoarsely, a sort of strange glee in her voice. "To see how it works out this time. It goes around and around. Money and rumor and love."

She gave Dare a mysterious smile. "I was once beautiful," she said. "More beautiful than you." Then she put her cane to the floor and hobbled off, Dare and McFee following.

She stopped by the front door and stared up at Dare. "Money isn't everything, my dear," Mrs. Bailey warned, but her eyes glittered strangely. "Remember that."

She moved past Dare with surprising swiftness, opened the screen door and stepped onto the porch.

"She's having one of her spells," Mr. McFee said pettishly. "Otherwise you wouldn't be getting off so easily. I still say you presented yourself falsely, and I do not like the idea of a woman of scandal linked to one of my clients, especially one of the moral fiber of Tabitha Bailey. The reputation of this place is important to her. I trust you can force yourself, temporarily, at least, to live up to the high standards she has always set. Do not offend her. She is a woman who can afford to indulge her whims."

"You wanted some money?" Dare asked, eager to be rid of him. She watched Mrs. Bailey standing on the porch, leaning heavily on her cane and looking out moodily across the mountains.

Mr. McFee nodded briskly, and Dare finally set down Limburger and scribbled out a check. She placed it in Mr. McFee's seamed hand. She didn't walk him to the porch, but watched through the screen door as he guided the old woman down the stairs.

"I was beautiful once," she heard Mrs. Bailey say querulously. "I was more beautiful than she is."

"I'm sure you were," replied Mr. McFee obsequiously, opening the door of the ancient Dodge with a courtly flourish. "But I thought you fully intended to raise the rent—"

"Oh, be quiet," commanded Mrs. Bailey. "I wanted to see her, that's all. I do not like her. I do not like anyone these days. But she interests me. This house and this mountain do things to people, you know. I am curious what they will do to her."

Mr. McFee sighed in disgust. He kicked ineffectually at a tuft of grass, then climbed into the car.

"Now what was that about?" Dare asked Limburger, as she watched the old Dodge huff and rattle away.

She frowned. Oliver McFee had learned who she was and smelled opportunity—opportunity to make money or trouble or both. And Mrs. Bailey had seemed to be cut from exactly the same cloth—at first.

But Dare felt with strange certainty that the old woman had indeed come to see her, to judge her. What had she said? That she wanted Dare to stay because she wanted to see what happened this time. That the house and the mountain did things to people. What could she possibly mean by that?

And the old woman had warned her that money wasn't everything. Strange, it was just the opposite of what Fawn had always told her. And, why did such a peculiar light come into her eyes when she talked about the DuLongs?

She had sensed envy in her words. Envy and regret and a certain longing...though for what Dare could not imagine.

But she understood instinctively the truth of one thing Mrs. Bailey had said. A man like Rip DuLong would never care for anything more than his precious land. A man like him could easily rend a feminine heart apart forever. Dare had read a poem once that said it was painful to weep over a cruel man, but it was far worse when a kind and laughing one made you cry.

CHAPTER SEVEN

DARE DREADED her weekly shopping trip into Arcadia. It was Friday, and the new issues of the *World Sun* and other tabloids would glare at her from the stands.

She hoped Warren had taken her seriously, and the story of her marriage to Sullivan had been retracted. But she had her doubts. At the very least, she crossed her fingers that there would be no further word on it—that he and Sullivan would let the story die a natural death. Then, when the story had fled from people's minds, they could break the so-called engagement with a minimum of fuss and no loss of face to Sullivan.

From some of the bold or curious glances she received as she went about her errands, she knew that Billy Bob had been right—people now recognized her. But as Billy Bob had said, they still seemed friendly and unaffected by the knowledge. They treated her as he said they would—as if she was simply one of the folks.

"Howdy. Miss Sheffield, isn't it?" said the elderly attendant at a service station where she stopped. "Hope you like it down here. We're all mighty fond of this part of the country. Hope you enjoy your stay."

"I know you," said the woman at the bookstore, where Dare stopped to buy a cookbook. "I've seen your picture. Welcome to the valley. I've been here fifteen years. I couldn't call another place home. Never get me back to the city—no, ma'am."

"Well, hi, honey," piped a waitress in the café where she stopped for a cup of coffee. "I heard you was down here. Aim to stay a spell?" The waitress seemed the most curious of the three.

"Could be." She smiled. "You never know."

"Sorry about your mama," she said with what seemed like genuine sympathy. "I read about it in the papers. It's right hard to have sickness like that in the family."

She said nothing more, but gave Dare a free refill on coffee. Dare watched her scurry away, feeling slightly numbed. How few people had said that to her, she thought. "Sorry about your mother." Yet here, in Arcadia, a perfect stranger uttered it, and did so with feeling.

In the supermarket, she eyed the rack of fresh tabloids with trepidation, but saw her name on none. She sighed with relief, but bought the newest copy of the *World Sun*, just to make sure no stories were buried inside.

She carried the groceries to the car, got in, took the paper, and began scanning it. If the story was retracted or dead, she would be safe. She could avoid confrontation with Warren and Sullivan and the fearsome powers of the gossip press. And she could avoid confrontation with Rip. She would prove herself right—if you leave things alone, they'll just go away.

Then in the center section titled "Celeb News 'N' Views," she found the story she had dreaded. It was short, almost a snippet. But it was enough.

She reread the article, grinding her teeth in frustration. The familiar feeling of angry sickness assailed her. Sullivan was quoted as saying that the big day would be soon. And that she was still in Paris spending up a storm on designer originals for her trousseau.

Drat Sullivan! she thought—how far did he think he could push her? And drat Warren, too. Did they think she was nothing but clay they could mold into any shape they wanted? And drat the *World Sun*. It made her sound like a pleasure-mad brat, living high and lavishly in the City of Light. Lies and more lies. As usual the *World Sun* was stuffed with them.

She looked warily at the pay phone outside the supermarket. Suddenly it didn't seem private enough for what she had to do.

She drove to the small florist shop on Main Street. It also served as the local telegraph office. Billy Bob had explained he delivered a lot more flowers than telegrams, and that he puttered around the shop a lot more than he delivered at all. He was officially retired, working for his niece, Flora, the florist.

She went into Flora's with a little too much desperation in her step and in her eyes. The woman—tall and thin, stared at her with mild alarm.

"Can I help you, honey? Is something wrong?"

"Is Billy Bob here?" Dare asked, her voice knotted.

"He sure is, honey. He's in the greenhouse." She called for him.

Billy Bob ambled in from the adjoining greenhouse, wiping potting soil from his hands. "Why, hey there, Miss Sheffield," he smiled. "You finally decide to answer all them telegrams?"

"No," she said, blushing. "I was wondering if you had—well—a private phone I could use. Really private. It won't cost you anything. I have a credit card."

"Sheffield?" said Flora, recognition dawning on her long face. "Oh! You're *her*."

"I told you, Flora," Billy Bob said sternly. "The girl's just folks, same as anybody. Somethin' wrong, honey?"

She took a deep breath. "The papers are telling lies about me again," she said, wishing she could cry. "I have to talk to somebody. I have to put this straight."

Flora came out from behind the counter. "If you're talkin' about the paper I think you're talkin' about, honey, pay no never-mind. Everybody knows there's no truth in it. But you come in my office. There's a phone in there."

She led Dare into a tiny office, pulled out the desk chair, left her and closed the door. Dare started dialing. She didn't notice the bouquet of yellow daisies on the desk or the bristling bulletin board.

She heard the distant switches and hums as the operator tried to connect her to Warren's number. Then she heard the slightly blurred recording:

"The number you have dialed is no longer in service," said the voice. "Consult information."

Impossible, thought Dare, and asked the operator to check the number again. But there was no mistake. Warren's office phone was disconnected. Feeling a wave of apprehension, she asked to be connected to his home number. She listened to the switching and the humming of the circuits again.

Just when she thought she had made contact, the precise and muted voice of a recording droned in her ear again.

"The number you have dialed is no longer in service. Consult information."

Frightened, Dare asked the operator if there was a listing for Warren Kroger or Kroger Enterprises. There was none.

Where was Warren? she thought in panic. Why had he cut off his phones? What was going on? She sat, nibbled on her thumbnail for a moment, then tried to call Sullivan's office. It took her forever to get through.

At last she was connected to a voice she recognized—Tiffany, the secretary of Sullivan's publicist.

"Sheffy?" she asked disapprovingly. "It's about time. I'll connect you to Vernon. It'll take a minute. He's in an important conference."

Vernon Calderone was Sullivan's publicist, a man whose unblinking coolness Fawn had always admired. Dare listened to recorded music for what seemed an interminable time before he finally picked up the phone.

"Where the hell are you?" Vernon demanded without preliminary. He had a voice as hard as concrete. "Are you in Manhattan?"

"No," she said, her voice breathy from nervousness. "I want to talk to Sullivan. I want this story on the marriage killed—I don't want to see any more about it."

"Yeah?" Vernon asked. "Maybe you better come back and tell him yourself, sister. Better yet, maybe you should come back and do what he tells you. I mean it. You're causing trouble. We're covering for you, Sheffy, but don't make my job any tougher than it is."

"Make your job tough?" she asked in disbelief. "Where's Sullivan? I want to talk to Sullivan. And where's Warren? I can't get in touch with him. What's going on?"

"Sullivan's busy," Vernon snapped. "He's getting ready for a tour—remember? He hasn't got time to play games with you. And he doesn't want to talk to you till you start acting like an adult. Now get back here."

"Where's Warren?" she asked, beginning to feel as if she were trapped in a nightmare. "I have to talk to him."

"I'd like to talk to Warren myself," Vernon growled. "I don't know where he is. He's disappeared. You got trouble, Sheffy—big trouble. Now get back here. Sullivan will explain."

"You explain," she demanded.

"I wouldn't if I could," Vernon replied venomously. "You think I'm being told everything? All I know is I smell trouble—lots of it—and the only message I got for you from Sullivan is for you to get back here and do what you're told. I don't know what's going on, but I know you're at the center of it. So be a good girl, like old times, all right?"

She clenched the receiver so tightly her knuckles paled. "You," she said very carefully, "tell Sullivan if he has any messages for me he can give them to me himself. In the meantime, I'm calling the press and stopping this nonsense."

Vernon's voice became ominous. "Do that, Sheffy, and kiss everything goodbye. I mean it. You'll stir up more damnation than you ever believed existed. That much I know. Keep that beautiful mouth shut, just like always."

"Vernon!" she panicked.

"I mean it. Get back, and in the meantime, keep quiet. Or I have a feeling all our phones are going to be disconnected—not just Warren's. You'll have blood on your hands. Lots of it."

He hung up.

She listened to the sinister hum of the line for a moment. She stared unseeing at the ridiculously cheerful yellow of the daisies on the desk. At last she hung up.

She came out of the office feeling numb, her knees slightly weak. "Sorry to tie up your phone for so long," she apologized to Flora. Billy Bob still stood by the counter, his sagging face concerned.

"You all right?" he asked.

"Fine," she said weakly.

"Honey," Flora said, studying her with dark eyes. "I know this is none of my business. I hate to admit I even read some of those papers. I only do at the hairdresser's—but if somebody's trying to push you around, don't let 'em. From what I read, seems people been runnin' your life long enough. You stick to your guns, honey, hear me?"

"Oh, hush, Flora," Billy Bob said impatiently. "Leave her be. Don't go pushin' into her private business."

"I'm not pushin'," Flora said, looking down her nose at Billy Bob. "I am expressin' an opinion. It's a free country." She looked at Dare again. "Come in anytime, darlin'. Glad to be of help. But you remember what I said—don't let anybody push you around."

Dare's head whirred crazily all the way home. Where was Warren? Why had he cut off his phones? He had warned her there was trouble—but could the trouble be so serious he had fled from it? It seemed impossible.

Her conversation with Vernon had been more disturbing than enlightening. Why did he think he and Sullivan could manipulate her as if she were a puppet? Sullivan was acting like a spoiled crown prince, issuing orders, mandates, ultimatums through his underlings.

Yet for all of Vernon's rudeness, his snapping of orders, he seemed puzzled by what was going on, too. He also sounded frightened, and men such as Vernon didn't frighten easily.

Perhaps Rip was right, she thought nervously. Perhaps she should have called the press immediately, ending the charade once and for all. It would have been honest. It would have freed her from this distressing situation—wouldn't it?

But Vernon made her feel that to do so would not only be foolish, it would be dangerous—dangerous to people besides herself.

She could come to only one conclusion. Whatever it was, whatever mess Warren and Fawn and Sullivan had created, she refused to take part in it. If Sullivan expected anything at all from her, he could get in touch with her. He could explain. He owed her that much. If what was going on was really that important, he'd find her. She was sick of the mystery, sick of the threats. Let the next move be his.

Besides, she thought in perplexity, he didn't want to marry her anyway, had never wanted to marry her. So why was marriage suddenly such an important issue to him?

She thought of Rip, her heart contracting. He wouldn't understand about this latest story in the *World Sun*. He would despise her for not taking charge of her own life. He would be reminded that she was like his mother—naive and helpless. He would never understand why she couldn't have the story retracted.

With a sickening jolt, she realized that what terrified her most of all in the whole mess was that Rip wouldn't understand—that he might never understand. It terrified her because Rip was becoming...she refused to think of what he was becoming to her. She would not dwell on her gray-eyed neighbor with his devil-may-care smile. Thinking of him would make the whole situation more painful than she could bear.

The gloomy weather seemed to intensify her distress. Gray clouds lowered until the tops of the distant mountains were invisible. The sky seemed to clamp down like a lid. No breezes cooled the mountain; all the colors looked different, strange. Even the normally cheerful red of the sumac in the wild fields now looked transformed, almost sinister.

Dare struggled to master a rented carpet-shampooer, and Limburger, exiled to the front porch, paced nervously and whined at intervals.

She spent the rest of the afternoon in desultory experiment with the cookbook, making a tuna casserole, then creating a marvelous mess as she struggled to make chocolate chip cookies.

She was so dusted with flour when she finished that she looked like a ghost, and a week before she would have delighted in the humor of it. But today the pleasure felt hollow. She had tried to leave her old life, but it followed her like some beast of prey stalking in wait.

She ate supper without appetite, nibbled without enthusiasm at a warm cookie. She went out on the porch, taking a cup of coffee for herself and a cookie for Limburger. He had disappeared, probably gone hunting, disgusted at being shut out of the house all afternoon. She sat in the swing moodily, forcing herself to eat the cookie. It was a good cookie for her first try, she thought with irony.

She had no problem at all keeping up with the housework, as old and dusty as the house was. It came to her as naturally as breathing. But then Fawn had always scolded her that she had "an ordinary mentality." Once Fawn had said, "I swear, you're happier watching the pigeons in the park than putting on a million dollars worth of jewelry and getting your picture taken. Do you realize if it weren't for me, you'd just be common?"

For a girl with a common mentality, she was at the center of a most uncommon situation.

The sky was darkening fast, the sunset barely coloring the thick, fast-moving clouds. Far on the misty horizon she could see weird glimmers of lightning. The air itself felt ominous, charged. Sometimes an alien gust of wind flared coldly, and the leaves on the mulberry tree showed their pale undersides. Dust lifted and flew from the lane.

She wondered if Rip would come, then realized he wouldn't. He'd have read about her in the tabloid today and he'd be disgusted with her for letting the situation get so out of hand.

What did it matter anyway? she thought rebelliously, drawing her knees up under her chin. It wasn't as if he wanted to marry her. He'd made it clear that commitment was the furthest thing from his mind. All he wanted to do was take her to bed. He probably resented Sullivan out of some primal, male urge that found its roots in pride, not affection.

She shouldn't think about Rip at all. Everything would be easier if he hadn't come along. He probably considered every unattached woman who rented this house fair game. What did they call it? *Les droits du signeur*—the rights of the master.

The chill wind gusted again. A longer glimmer in the sky and a low growl of thunder told her the storm was moving closer.

She whistled for Limburger, but he didn't come. Maybe he was hiding in the barn, she thought. She'd heard dogs were frightened of storms.

Then, through the gloom, she saw the lights of Rip's truck coming up the lane, and she stood, waiting for him, her heart beating fast.

He stopped the truck and got out. He looked tired. She glanced at her watch. He was later than usual. He must have put in an extraordinarily long day. Maybe, she thought with childish hope, he hadn't seen the story.

Things were taut enough between them without this new complication.

He took off his hat as he came up the porch stairs. He ran a hand through the waves of his thick brown hair. He sank wearily in the swing then looked up at her wryly.

"Sit down," he commanded. "It makes me tired to look at somebody standing up."

She settled beside him nervously. "Long day?" she asked, wanting to reach out and smooth his hair back from his brow.

"About ninety-eight hours," he sighed harshly. "The harvester broke down."

"Did you get it running again?" she asked, concerned. He looked as if he was pushing himself too hard and too far.

"Yes. And I'm the lucky man on the crew. I left early. The others'll go till the rain hits. We've got another day at the most to get this crop in."

"Why do you work so hard?" she asked, studying the weariness in his strong face. "Everybody says you've made a success of the place. Can't you just sit back and—and manage or something?"

"Not enough of a success," he said shortly. "Not yet. Someday I can slow down—until then, like I told you, I'm married to this mountain—damn it."

"But you love it," she commented, staring out at the lightning in the distance. The truth hurt her. *The land was all he loved.*

"I don't love what's about to happen," he said darkly. He tossed his head meaningfully at the foreboding sky. Another gust of wind came, ruffling his hair.

"The rain," she said, suddenly understanding. "Will it hurt the grapes?"

"Probably," he said without emotion. "If the storm doesn't damage them, mildew might. That I can't help, so I don't worry about it. You, however, are another matter."

"Me?" she asked in unhappy surprise.

"You." He dug into the hip pocket of his closely fitted jeans. "You I always have to worry about. I stopped by the house to get you some fresh flashlight batteries. I'm not so sure the ones you've got aren't dead. Like me at the moment. Here."

She took the batteries and looked down at them. "You always think of everything," she said softly.

His reply was curt. "The hell I do." He looked at her, his lean face inscrutable. "We're in for a spell of weather, sure enough. It gets wild up on this mountain. You can come over to my place if you want. It's all perfectly proper. Tessie, my housekeeper, is the most stout-hearted of chaperones."

His invitation had been as impersonal as if he had extended it to a maiden aunt.

"No thanks," she said uneasily.

"You want me to stay?" he asked, the same indifference in his tone.

"Of course not," she answered as lightly as she could. "I'll be fine. I'm not scared of a little rain."

They sat for a moment in uncomfortable silence. "Where's Limburger?" he asked at last, looking around.

"At first I thought he was off pouting," she explained, glad for a neutral topic. "I shampooed the carpets and locked him out for a while. Now I think maybe he's hiding from the storm."

"When you find him, keep him in," Rip ordered brusquely.

She felt a patter of alarm in her chest. "Why?"

"Because among other things that have gone wrong today, there was a wild dog spotted near the fields. It could be rabid. This is mad-dog weather."

"A mad dog?" she asked in alarm.

"Possibly," he said, in the same gruff voice. "There are always wild dogs in the country. But they're wary. This one didn't act right. I sent one of the men to look at the far field. He saw the dog and took a couple of shots at it. He hit it, but he didn't kill it. The thing lit into the woods."

"But—" Dare said, trying to reassure herself "—Limburger's safe, isn't he? He's had his rabies shot."

"The rabies wouldn't kill him," Rip said sarcastically. "The dog would. It was a big dog, Dare. Once you find that mutt of yours, keep him in. Stick close to the house yourself. Don't go wandering around."

"I'm not in the habit of wandering around," she said tartly. "But maybe I should be. I should be out looking for him. How do I know he isn't in trouble already?"

She started to rise, but Rip's hand clamped on her wrist, pulling her back into the swing. "I said—don't go wandering around. And don't worry about your dog. He's smart. He's probably fine. The other dog's hurt. He's slowed down considerably. He might be dead, for all I know. But until I know, do as I say, damn it!"

"Rip," she cried in protest, "you're hurting me!"

He released her wrist so quickly there was almost insult in the gesture.

"You don't like being ordered around, right?" he snapped.

She nodded, unsure of herself.

"Well, I no longer give a damn what you like or don't like," he continued, giving her a glance that was more threatening than the nearing lightning flashes. "If you want to come to the country to play hide-and-seek, or to make your city friends chase you down, fine. Play all those games all you want. But get this through your head: *When Nature plays games, it plays for keeps.* Listen to what I tell you, and do what I say."

Her patience, tried long and harshly all day, snapped. "Oh, heavens!" she exclaimed angrily. "You sound like this is the jungle and you're the Great White Hunter. What do you want me to do? Say, 'Yes, Master,' and salaam to you?"

"No," he snipped back. "I want you to settle in for a storm like you've never seen, and don't blame me if it scares your lingerie off. I want you and your dog to be careful for the next few days. In the meantime, be aware that I'll be extremely glad when you get a phone, so I can have Tessie call to make sure you haven't got yourself in some mess, and I don't have to come running over here twice a day to make sure you're still alive."

"Nobody ever asked you to come over here!" she returned, wounded. "Who asked you to come over? I didn't."

"Human decency demands I keep an eye on you," he said sarcastically. "Besides, somebody's got to keep you safe for your precious bleached-blond boyfriend."

"He's not my boyfriend," she insisted hotly. "I suppose you saw that—that stupid story. It's the same as usual—a pack of lies."

"Yes, I saw the story," he answered sharply. "And yes, you keep saying it's a lie. In private. In public you let people say otherwise. But you're not doing one damn thing about it. It's not the way to gain confidence, Brown Eyes. Least of all from me. How many times do I have to tell you?"

"I'm trying to work it all out—at my own pace," she said with spirit, but she was beginning to feel extremely vulnerable.

"Have you even bothered to find out what the problem is with this Warren?" he taunted.

"I don't know what the problem is," she answered, shaking her head in frustration. If she could explain to him about the phones being disconnected, about Warren's disappearance, about Vernon's warnings, maybe Rip would not be so scalding, so judgmental.

But he gave her no chance. "Have you called anybody to cancel this so-called phony engagement?"

"I can't call anybody yet," she tried to explain. "I really can't—"

He rose, and chucked her under the chin flippantly. "Either you're lying, darlin'—" he gave a short laugh "—or you're too immature to face facts. Or you enjoy making a circus of your life. And I don't want to be a clown in anybody's circus. I told you before, I don't play games. Especially tonight. I'm too tired. So long. Don't let the wind blow you away."

He strode down the stairs and got into his truck. She rose and went to the edge of the steps.

"Rip DuLong!" she cried. "You don't even listen. You're as bad as everybody else!"

"I'm probably worse." There was bitter mockery in his voice. "After all, what am I promising you? Nothing—except the chance to stand on your own two feet and take chances like a real woman. I guess you'd rather be a tease."

He switched on his lights, started the truck. He backed up sharply, then sped down the lane.

She threw the flashlight batteries as hard as she could into the forsythia bushes.

"I hate you," she shouted with vehemence, into the storm-heavy air. "If I told you a thousand times, I couldn't tell you how much I hate you."

But even as she said the words, she knew she didn't hate him. Quite the contrary. She was falling in love with him, she realized with a sickening lurch. And it hurt just as much as Fawn always warned it would.

What's more, she had acted like a child, had been incapable of explaining her predicament. She went down the stairs and began to search through the forsythia bushes for the flashlight batteries, feeling all this turmoil was a judgment on her. Everyone had been right—Fawn, Sullivan, Warren, Rip. She couldn't take care of herself.

No. That wasn't right, she vowed. She wouldn't give up. She wouldn't go back. She wouldn't do as she was told. She would do things her own way and show them all.

Cursing her dilemma, she groped among the stalks of the forsythia for the batteries but couldn't find them. She stopped searching when the first chill drops of rain came pelting down. They fell so hard they stung.

CHAPTER EIGHT

RIP HAD BEEN RIGHT about the storm. It swept the mountain like a Titan's wrath.

Dare sat huddled on the love seat, her bathrobe pulled around her tightly. The storm ranted with a force she could never have imagined.

She had watched it from the porch awhile, hoping Limburger would show. He didn't. The lightning and thunder had drawn nearer. As she'd watched the jagged spears flash and felt the rising wind, she grew frightened and went inside. She had seen the lights of distant towns eerily snuffed out by the storm's fury, like candles being blown out.

The house lights flickered repeatedly. Thunder boomed so loudly the windows shuddered in their panes. She had candles ready, stuck in empty bottles, matches in her pocket and Rip's flashlight beside her. The batteries hadn't died, thankfully.

The wind blew maniacally in spurts, then would go weirdly still. She'd switched on the portable radio Rip had given her, and heard weather warnings in broken chatter. But the storm created so much static and interference she was afraid the radio would explode.

Another bolt of lightning turned the night sky white. Thunder crashed loudly enough to shake the walls. She shivered. She wished she had swallowed her pride and gone with Rip to his house. She wished she had asked him to stay. She wished she had looked for Limburger while it was still light and had him beside her on the love seat, so she could hug him for comfort.

The wind rose wildly, shrieking, and lightning struck so close the thunder crashed simultaneously.

Dare jumped involuntarily. The lights went out. Everything was dark, black.

She wondered with alarm how close the bolt had struck. She had a panicky image of the house in flames. What could she do, isolated as she was with no phone, if there was a fire? She remembered Rip's warning that Nature played for keeps. She was beginning to understand.

Shakily she struck a match and lit two of the candles. Their dancing light gave a deceptively warm glow to the room.

The rain seemed to be slowing a bit. The wind stopped. There was the steady drumming of water on the house, then another flash and crash that made her jump.

She steeled herself, got up, and opened the door, looking outside. She saw nothing. For the first time she realized how absolutely dark the country was.

She stood on the porch, looking into the seamless blackness. The lights in the valley were still out. Lightning had robbed the night of all light except its own.

She shivered. Then she heard barking, faint but insistent. She clutched her robe more tightly around her body and listened, straining to hear.

It was Limburger's bark—the one that signaled an intruder. It sounded angry, but unusually frightened, almost demented. It came from the barn.

The mad dog, she thought. *The mad dog is in the barn. It's hidden in the barn, and Limburger's found it. And it'll kill him.*

Her isolation and her helplessness overwhelmed her. Limburger's yappings grew louder, more frantic. Then the wind gusted again and carried them away.

She ran inside, grabbed the flashlight and ran into the bedroom. She tugged on her jeans, boots, a sweater, then snatched her raincoat and went into the kitchen. She opened a top cupboard and took out the gun.

It felt heavy and awkward in her hand. She realized she hated the thing, but she had been right to keep it.

Dare went outside and stood hesitantly on the porch, trying to see through the driving rain. Again she heard Limburger's berserk barking.

What should she do? she wondered. Should she go running through the rain like some woman in a horror movie? She didn't want to go to that barn. She didn't want to face what was up there.

She took a deep breath.

Calm down, she told herself. It was probably nothing. Rip had said the mad dog was wounded, maybe dead. A stray cat may have hidden in the barn to get out of the rain. Or a skunk or a possum. She had a gun. She was safe. She'd just go up there and get Limburger and bring him back.

Reluctantly, Dare set out through the darkness for the barn. The flashlight showed only weakly now, and she cursed herself for flinging the batteries away.

"Limburger, you mutt," she said to herself, "I hope you appreciate this, because I'm scaring myself to death."

The rain drenched her hair, pounded through her silky city raincoat, plastering it to her body. She was only halfway to the barn and already her boots were soaked through.

The lightning flashed, farther away now, but for a moment it made the barn stand out against the sky, a black hulk. Limburger's bark sounded closer now, more furious.

Whatever was in there hadn't hurt him, she told herself. It probably wasn't dangerous. She'd just grab the dog and take him back to the house.

She called for him, but he didn't come. He only barked louder. *I don't want to do this,* she thought, swinging the barn door open. *It's probably nothing,* another part of her mind insisted. He had probably found a mouse or a chipmunk or a bird.

The dim ray of the flashlight cast shadows as she moved inside. The barn, so harmless, so comforting by day, was transformed by darkness. It seemed alive with creaks and shudders and rattles. It seemed haunted.

"Limburger!" she called, her voice stern. "You come home. Stop this!"

She could not see him; she could only hear him. Then the light caught him, crouched low in one of the stalls, his back hair bristling.

At the same moment she heard another sound, the low, agonized growl of a larger dog.

"Limburger!" she screamed. She saw the shadow of the bigger dog feint at him, growling more loudly.

The mad dog, she thought in terror. *Shoot it. Shoot it before it gets us both.*

She fumbled to get a grip on the gun. She lost her hold on the flashlight. It clattered to the floor. She could barely see the two growling shadows in the stall.

Her hands shook badly. She aimed toward the larger shadow. She squeezed the trigger.

Nothing happened.

She could see the larger dog feinting again at Limburger, then it barked savagely at her. She squeezed the trigger again. It didn't yield.

The safety catch. The safety catch was still on, she thought. The hammer, she was supposed to cock the hammer.

She pulled back the hammer. It snapped. The gun was like a lump of blackness in the shadows. Frantically she fumbled with it, feeling for the safety catch.

Then the big dog lunged.

She felt for the trigger frantically and the gun seemed to come alive in her hand. There was a crash as loud as a thunderclap. There was pain. There was darkness.

RAIN PELTING HER FACE woke her. That and the swearing. She tried to open her eyes, but the rain stung. Strong arms held her, and she had a terrible certainty that she was being borne off by the Angel of Death.

Except angels didn't swear.

"Am I alive?" she asked, then shook her head feebly, trying to escape the rain.

"Yes, not that you deserve to be."

It was Rip's voice, angry, disgusted and disapproving. It sounded wonderful.

Weakly she put her arms around his neck.

"What happened?" she asked, laying her face against his chest.

"You shot yourself in the knee, Miss I-can-take-care-of-myself. You're lucky you didn't blow your head off."

She suddenly realized her knee hurt, badly.

He was carrying her up the porch stairs. "Where's Limburger?" she asked, suddenly frightened again. "The mad dog—Rip—it was in the barn!"

"Limburger's right behind us," he snapped, kicking the front door open. He swore again.

He carried her into the bedroom and dumped her, rather unceremoniously, onto her bed.

He had a large flashlight, and he shone the beam on her leg. The left knee of her jeans was pierced neatly.

"I think you only creased yourself," he said pulling her boots off.

Her knee stung and throbbed. With a single, expert movement Rip tore her jeans, baring her leg almost to the hip.

She was afraid to look. She supposed she was hopelessly mangled. Then she glimpsed the wound through her lashes, and saw that it was only a nick, a red line on the outer edge of her knee.

Rip examined it critically, then bound his handkerchief around it to stop the bleeding. She winced.

She could see a bedraggled Limburger eyeing her guiltily from the bedroom doorway.

Rip swore again, left the room, taking one of the candles. She heard him cursing and rummaging in the bathroom.

He returned, removed the hanky and began swabbing her knee and pouring antiseptic on it.

"Ouch!" she gasped.

"Ouch, indeed," he scoffed. "Be quiet. You deserve to hurt."

"The dog—" she said, feeling slightly drunken. "The mad dog. Did you kill it?"

"There wasn't any mad dog," he returned gruffly, wrapping gauze around her knee.

"Rip, there was!" she insisted. He tightened the gauze and she grimaced. "I saw it. It was huge. It tried to get Limburger—and me."

"Bullfeathers," he snorted. "To put it politely."

"I saw it," she repeated. "It was enormous!"

The lights flickered on, went out, flickered again, then finally stayed on. Rip blew out the candle, switched off his flashlight. He wound tape expertly around the gauze and cut it with his jackknife.

"The enormous and horrible mad dog you saw," he said contemptuously, "is a perfectly sane and medium-sized hound. Abandoned, yes. Mad, no he wasn't trying to attack you. *She* was trying to defend her pups. Which the poor creature just had. Congratulations. You no longer have one dog. You have thirteen."

"What?" she asked incredulously, sitting up straighter.

He was sitting next to her on the bed. He started unbuttoning her sodden rain coat. His coat glistened with water, and his hair was curly from the rain.

"Yes," he said with a curt nod. He stripped off her raincoat. "You have thirteen dogs. This troublemaker here—" he indicated the disheveled and repentant Limburger "—and twelve more in the barn. Eleven pups. A fine litter. Again, congratulations. You're an aunt."

He threw her raincoat into the large wicker basket at the foot of the bed. "Get out of those clothes," he ordered. "Get into your nightgown. If you don't die of bullet wounds, you'll die of pneumonia. The bed's getting soaked."

She tried gingerly to raise herself. "I don't know if I can walk."

"Then hop. Damn it."

For once, she didn't resent his orders. Meekly she hung up her jeans and took her nightgown from the closet. He sat on the bed, glowering at her.

She grabbed her robe and hobbled into the bathroom to change, then came out, hugging her robe tightly around herself.

He had hung up their raincoats and changed the sheets.

"Get in," he ordered, turning back the covers.

Self-consciously she took off her robe and draped it over the end of the bed. Favoring her hurt knee, she climbed between the sheets.

He had pulled up a chair beside the bed. He switched off the light and sat down.

"What are you doing?" she asked in a small voice.

"I'm staying. Be quiet."

"You don't have to stay. And I don't think I can sleep anyway. My heart's pounding too hard."

"I'm not leaving you alone. You could wake up in a panic. You probably will. Now be quiet."

She could feel his presence through the darkness as if she were bound to him.

She was quiet for a long moment.

"Why did you come?" she asked softly. "How did you find me?"

"I knew the lightning hit close to you. I came to check. Then I heard the barking in the barn, and I found you, lying on the floor like a sack of cornmeal. Now hush."

She hushed momentarily, but couldn't stay still. "I did think it was the mad dog, Rip," she said at last.

"That's what makes me craziest of all," he grumbled. "I'll give you credit. You may be foolhardy, but at least you're brave."

"I wasn't brave. I was scared to death."

"That's what brave is. Doing something even if you're scared to death. Be quiet. Go to sleep."

She pulled the sheets up tightly around her neck. She thought of how uncomfortable he must be, sitting in the darkness on the hard chair.

"I—the gun jammed," she murmured. She supposed she was trying to apologize, to explain away her foolhardiness. "I couldn't get the safety catch off."

He groaned. "I don't believe this."

"It's true," she said. "I couldn't get the safety catch off. Then I guess it misfired or something."

"Dare," he said, disgust in his voice. "There isn't any safety catch on a revolver. Only automatics have safeties. As soon as you cocked that gun, it had a hair trigger. I told you a hundred times that if you don't understand guns, don't fool with them. I hope you've learned your lesson. Maybe you're beyond learning, I don't know."

An unhappy moan escaped her. Her ignorance of the gun seemed like some final, fatal blow. She had juggled it around in the semidarkness, cocked, looking for a safety catch that didn't exist. She might have killed herself. He had been right, as usual, and she couldn't blame him for being disgusted. She was profoundly disgusted with herself. She felt a hot tear course down her cheek, then another.

"Dare?" he asked gruffly.

She didn't answer.

"Are you crying?" His voice was still hard.

She could not answer him.

"I said—are you crying?" he demanded in exasperation.

Suddenly he was beside her, holding her in his arms, kissing the tears away.

She clung to him.

"I don't think this is the way to get you to sleep," he said huskily.

He stretched out beside her. He cradled her tightly.

"I don't care," she whispered through her tears. "Hold me. Please just hold me."

He held her more closely.

"Shh," he said, kissing her mouth. "Shh." He kissed her again.

She put her arms around his neck, tried to hold him closer still.

"I didn't mean to make you cry," he said, running his fingers through her damp hair. "Oh, Dare, you smell like the summer and the rain. And you're trembling. Don't. Don't."

"I'm such a fool," she said against his cheek.

"I didn't mean to talk to you like that," he whispered. "You know why I do it, don't you?"

"Because I deserved it?"

"No," he breathed. "You didn't deserve it at all. I do it because . . ."

He kissed her again, and her heart careened away.

"Because," he murmured against her lips. "Never mind why. I just do it—because."

She let herself sink into the warmth of his touch, the pleasure and excitement of his nearness.

But he did not kiss her again. Instead, he put his hand on her nape and laid her face against his chest. She could feel the hard, steady beat of his heart.

The muscles in his arms lost none of their tenseness, but somehow his hold on her gentled. He took a deep breath.

"I want to make love to you," he said.

She was silent, frightened and yearning beside him.

He took another deep breath. "I would love to make love to you. But I won't."

She stayed quiet a moment, her heart dancing erratically. "We're in bed together," she said at last. "I asked you to hold me. I know what that means."

"You don't know what it means," he replied tersely. "But I'll hold you, Dare. I'll get you through the night."

"But why...?" she started to ask, wanting him to kiss her again.

"Because, my love, there are three of us in this bed. And one is named Sullivan. You know it as well as I do. He makes it very crowded. I may be amorous, but I'm not kinky."

"But," she protested. "I don't love him. I don't."

I love you, she wanted to say, but didn't have the courage. Nor did she have the courage or experience to kiss him, touch him in such a way that would make him change his mind.

"So you say," he said. "Maybe it's true. But it occurs to me that I'm in bed with a woman who's exhausted, hurt, upset, and—just incidentally—engaged to another man. Isn't getting shot and passing out enough excitement for one night? If you think losing your virginity will improve matters, you're wrong. You don't know what you're doing at all. Especially to me. Go to sleep. I assure you this is more difficult for me than it is for you."

Sullivan, she thought wearily. *Always Sullivan. And the rest of the crazy world Fawn had created.* She nestled her head against Rip's chest, too tired to argue.

"Of course," he whispered, "if you knew your own mind well enough, and were a free woman...and if you came out and asked me..."

"Oh, don't," she whispered unhappily. "Don't talk that way."

"Shhh," he said again. "Just sleep, Dare. I'll hold you. All night long."

Cradled against his strength, at last she slept.

SHE AWOKE in the morning with a sneeze. Another sneeze answered her from the kitchen.

Rain still drummed on the roof, slow now, and steady. In a moment, Rip was by her bedside, bringing her a cup of coffee.

"I'd have made you breakfast," he said. "But the last time I took a frying pan in hand they smelled the burning in three counties."

He was unshaven, his clothing wrinkled, and his wavy hair, uncombed, hung over his eyes. She thought he looked as handsome as ever.

She sneezed again. He handed her a tissue. "Ah, sin," he said. "We spent the night locked in each other's arms. Now our just punishment. I, of course, am too rugged to catch cold from mere rain. I sneeze as a result of sexual frustration."

She looked at him. He looked perfectly serious. She blushed. "Oh, dear," she said. "I'm sorry."

He sat down on the chair and laughed wryly. "You believed that? You are an innocent. You do need watching out for, m'dear."

She blushed harder. "Of course, I didn't believe it."

"Yes, you did. I saw the horror on your face. Never mind. Drink up. You're young and healthy. Your sneezes will disappear." She sat up and he handed her the coffee.

She took a sip. It was blissfully hot. "What about you?" she managed to say, not wanting to look at him. "Are you all right?"

He shrugged. "I'm healthy. I'll be fine by noon. How's the knee?"

"It doesn't hurt much."

She sipped her coffee, remembering the night before and feeling embarrassed.

"What are you looking so guilty about?" he asked. "You didn't do anything."

She met his gray gaze as levelly as she could. "I think that's thanks to you. You were right. I certainly wasn't myself last night."

Their eyes locked for a moment.

"I really hate myself," he said at last. "I should have ravished you properly, and shown you all the things the city boys don't know."

"Why didn't you?" she asked with surprising boldness. The electricity that crackled between them the night before hadn't vanished with the storm.

"I don't know," he said casually. "Maybe I thought if I held out, you'd come to me begging."

"Oh!" she said, and took a hasty sip of coffee to hide her humiliation. "You always say the most embarrassing things."

"I say what I think," he shrugged. "Besides, I figure why ruin what we have already?"

She cast him a wary look. "And just what do we have already?"

"A delightfully ambiguous relationship. You're an apparent innocent, searching for an idyll. I'm a simple country boy, searching for grim reality—what is truth? I ask myself repeatedly. Most specifically, what is the truth about you?"

"The truth about me is that I no longer know the truth nor probably ever did," she said.

She had awakened hungry, but her appetite fled. She finished her coffee in silence and set the cup on the scuffed bedside table. She reached for her robe, stood up self-consciously, and put it on, belting it tightly. She should tell him about her attempts to call Warren the day before. But she had to be calm, explain everything clearly. She desperately wanted him to know.

She passed her fingers through her hair. It was soft and unruly from the rain.

"I called Warren yesterday," she said. "Or tried to. He's had all his phones disconnected."

He looked at her, one eyebrow cocking sharply, his expression unreadable. "Interesting."

"I tried to talk to Sullivan and couldn't get him," she said, taking up her brush and beginning to brush her brown-gold hair. "I talked to his publicist. He wouldn't tell me anything. Except to practically threaten me to keep quiet and to come back."

"Threaten you?" he probed. His face still revealed nothing.

"He said—he hinted that a lot of people could be hurt," she said, putting down her brush. She had her back to him, but could see his reflection in the old dresser mirror.

"Fascinating," he said flippantly, as if none of it really mattered. "So why don't you go back to New York to investigate? Aren't you curious about all this intrigue?"

"No," she said shortly. She watched him in the mirror. "I'm frightened by it."

"So what do you plan to do?"

His eyes met hers in the mirror, and she dropped her glance. "I don't know. I'm surprised you're not telling me what to do. You always have."

He stood up and moved behind her. He put his hands on her shoulders. ''No. Not this time. From here on, you're on your own. The way you want to be. This is one subject on which I'm no longer giving out advice.''

Her body felt tingly at his touch, almost faint.

He watched her reflection in the mirror. ''Look at that face,'' he said, nodding at her image. His breath was warm against the side of her throat. ''Full of innocence and mystery. The first time I saw it I knew how those ancient Greek mortals felt when a goddess appeared before them.''

His right hand touched the tip of her chin then rested on her shoulder again. ''And yet—there's more to a woman than her face. Or other physical attributes, delectable as they may be. There's character, as well. There are the things she does—or doesn't do. There's the courage she has—or doesn't have.''

He raised her hair and kissed her nape. She shivered, and wanted to turn to him, yet she sensed the challenge in his words. What was she going to do about Sullivan? he was asking. What was she going to do about Warren? What was she going to do about him?

She closed her eyes.

His hands returned to her shoulders and tightened, ''Don't shut your eyes. Look at her.''

Obediently she opened her eyes, staring at the two of them in the mirror.

''She's the one who'll be making the decisions,'' Rip said, nodding at her reflection. ''She's the one who'll have to take action. That one. Right there. And I wonder what she'll do.''

''Nothing,'' she breathed, feeling helpless at his touch. ''Right now I can't do anything.''

He gave her shoulders a friendly squeeze then released her. "So be it," he said. "Who knows? Maybe your ostrich tactics are right. If you stick your head in the sand long enough, the trouble won't see you and will go away."

He stepped back, took his raincoat from the hook on the bedroom door, threw it over his arm.

She turned to face him. "I know you think I'm wrong—" she began.

He smiled sardonically. "No. Remember me? I'm the man who doesn't give advice anymore. Besides, I know how to treat your type."

She looked at him expectantly, hopefully. "How?" she breathed.

"The way all women should be treated. As recreational objects," he said, with a crooked smile. "What the hell. Life's too short to be serious. You came to play. All right. We'll play. No commitments to it, no future in it, no reason for it."

"Oh," she said, her chest tightening.

"And we'll have fun," he nodded. "What else is there to do? But now I must run along and tell lies to my housekeeper. I suppose now that I've stayed out all night, I've ruined my reputation forever, but what of that? Anything for a laugh, right?"

"Rip," she said in bewilderment, "I never know when you're serious or not—"

"I'm always serious about fun," he stated. He drew the curtain aside and peered out at the tapering rain. He put on his raincoat. "And don't go to the barn to play with the new puppies. From all appearances, that's another wild dog out there. She won't take your attentions kindly."

"But all those puppies—" she said, unhappy at seeing him ready to leave. "What do I do about all those puppies?"

His smile faded. "You're on your own, kid. And you've got to solve your own problems. Best of luck. By the way, I've got your gun." He patted the pocket of his raincoat. "Cheers," he said, then left.

She stared after him, feeling empty and resentful. What sort of man was he, so kind and sensitive one moment, so callous the next? And so lovable...

CHAPTER NINE

AFTER BREAKFAST she filled a mixing bowl with dog food, locked Limburger in the house and went to the barn, against Rip's advice.

The dog hadn't hurt her or Limburger, she reasoned. It had been as frightened, probably more so, than she. It was a poor abandoned creature, and it was most certainly hungry. She wasn't about to let it starve.

She approached it warily, babbling soothing words. The dog, brown and white, growled, but stayed faithfully by her puppies, trembling. Rip was right. There were eleven of the mites, blind, pug-nosed, mewling softly. There were brown ones, white ones, black ones and spotted ones.

The dog had made a nest out of old sacking under an overturned easy chair with the stuffing spilling out. Dare set the bowl down gently. When the dog began to eat, one eye suspiciously on its benefactor, Dare muttered, "Poor Stormy. I'll leave you alone now."

She left the barn, walked back to the house brooding, her hands in her raincoat pockets. The poor abandoned thing, she thought. Stormy was the perfect name for her.

Later she took her water. Again she growled, looked at her suspiciously, but refused to leave her pups. Dare spoke to her softly. She took an old milking stool, placed it at a distance from the dog, and sat watching her.

The dog obviously hadn't been around people for a while, and she had learned to fear them. Dare hoped patience would win her over. If being a model had taught her nothing else over all those years, it had taught her patience.

She went up to the barn again after supper. She took Stormy a few scraps. The dog already seemed to be getting used to her.

"We girls have to stick together," Dare told her solemnly, sitting on the milking stool. "Don't mind me. I'm just admiring your babies."

It was nearly dark when Rip found her in the barn. The dog growled at his entrance, slunk back farther beneath the old chair.

"I knew you'd be here," he said, standing tall in the doorway, "since it's precisely where I told you not to be."

"Shhh," she said softly. "You're scaring her. She's just starting to trust me."

She looked at the thin dog, quivering and growling at the figure in the door. "Don't mind him," she told Stormy. "He thinks I'm a recreational object, and he's been known to make the mockingbirds drunk, but other than that he's all right."

"Are you going to sit here all night long? Have you at last found a task to fulfill you—playing Florence Nightingale to a passel of pups?"

"Be quiet," Dare scolded softly. "You're upsetting her. No. I'm going back to the house."

She stood. He waited for her by the door, holding it open.

"How's your harvester?" she asked with exaggerated politeness. "In good health, I hope?"

"It's behaving. Unlike you. How's the knee?"

"It's behaving. Unlike you. Did the storm hurt the grapes?"

"Not much. We were lucky. No real damage done. But if this rain doesn't stop, there will be. Mildew will start."

"The farmer's life is not an easy one," she said crisply, climbing the porch stairs.

"Nor is it boring," he replied. "We found the mad dog, by the way. It was shot worse than we'd thought. It didn't make it through the night, poor devil. Now why don't you invite me inside and make me some coffee. After all—" he smiled at her "—I made yours this morning."

Limburger danced in welcome. Dare bustled about, trying to look efficient as she made coffee. She didn't want to think about this morning. Rip sat in one of the kitchen chairs, fondling Limburger's silky ears.

"Poor dog." He patted Limburger. "She's found someone new. She's ignoring you and me. All for some nasty old strays. I hope this teaches you a lesson about women. They're fickle."

Dare sat in the other chair. The coffee began to perk comfortingly.

He reached toward the plate of cookies on the table and helped himself. He bit into one. "Not bad," he said, his face judgmental. "You make these yourself? Pretty good, in fact. Want to get married? Oops, I forgot. You're already spoken for. Too bad."

"Stop that," she said moodily. "I'm not getting married. I told you that a million times. And you're not the marrying kind—remember?"

"All I know is what I read in the *World Sun*," he said mildly. "As for me not being the marrying kind—you're right. Not at this point, anyway."

"Not ever, I don't suppose," she said with forced lightness. "It would mean committing yourself to something other than your precious winery."

"I'm more serious than you know." He nodded curtly. "I've seen what building this place can do to a man. And a woman. My mother went without a lot of things. In fact, she went without just about everything. She was a woman who wanted and needed a lot more than she ever got. And my father hated himself for not being able to give it to her."

His face was meditative, controlled. "The crazy thing is they really loved each other. But she was fragile and had grown up so protected, it was hard for her to cope with things. The unhappier she became, the harder my father worked, hoping to make things better for her. And the harder he worked, the less she saw of him and the unhappier she became. What started out all sweetness and light became a long nightmare for both of them. I remember that. I remember it very clearly. It was a bad time. A long, bad time."

"But," Dare said carefully, as if making a casual point, "you overcame the obstacles. You've done so well."

He shrugged, frowning sardonically. "Not well enough. Maybe someday. Right now I'm taking a gamble on some new pinot grapes. Their yield is low but they're high in sugar. We've taken a bronze medal for our pinot noir in international competition. I want the gold. I want this place to be the number one winery in the South. Then there are a couple of California wineries I want to take on—and beat."

"Maybe you should marry a grape," Dare muttered.

"Maybe I should," he mused, his old lightness returning. "It wouldn't sass me. Are you really going to play nanny to all those mutts in the barn?"

"Yes," she said firmly. "Why not?"

"Because if anybody finds out, you'll be up to your pretty neck in dogs. People will come from all over to dump them here. There's a real problem with homeless dogs in the country."

"It's horrible," she said, still moody. "And she's not a bad-looking dog."

"No," he agreed. "She's got a lot of walker hound in her. She probably couldn't learn to hunt. So somebody dumped her. It happens all the time—like to this guy here." He scratched Limburger's ears again.

"I can't believe people can be so heartless."

"You've got a lot to learn."

The words hung heavily between them. It was the message he had given her often. She tried to ignore its overtones.

"They just abandon all these animals?" she asked.

He took another cookie. "Yup. And some starve, and some get hit, and some go wild. The wild ones learn to scavenge and to kill. They have to. But they become diseased, and have to be shot. What do you think you're going to do with that pack in the barn?"

"Find homes for them," she declared, rising to get the coffeepot.

"You really are a dreamer," he laughed. "Giving away dogs around here is like selling sand to the Arabs."

"I know a thing or two about getting things sold," she said, filling his cup. "I made a living helping getting things get sold—remember? I'll find them homes. You wait and see."

He laughed. "Maybe you will. You amaze me, Dare. How did your mother ever make you mind?"

She filled her cup, put the pot back on the stove and sat down again. "I don't want to talk about it," she murmured. Fawn's methods had been ancient and simple. She could make a person love her so much it hurt, then she could withhold her love. Adults understood this quickly. Dare had learned it slowly, painfully, and unwillingly.

"Not talking, eh?" he said lightly. "And the fabulous career she built for you—don't you even care about it?"

"At first it was fun," she admitted. "It was dressing up and making faces. Later it wasn't as much fun. Then it all became sort of awful. But I wanted to please her. She was never—"

"Satisfied?" he supplied, looking at her over the rim of his cup. His eyes were almost hard, measuring her reaction.

"She was never secure," Dare said softly. "That's all it was. She was never secure. Things had been too hard for her. She always was afraid the bad times would come back. That's why she drove herself."

"And kept the kid working," he said cynically. "So you had to postpone your childhood until now."

She stared into her cup. She supposed that's how she did appear to him—an indecisive, heedless child in a woman's body. Perhaps that was what she was. But she resented the remark.

"Maybe she wasn't so different from you," she said with a sudden bitter insight. "Whatever you get doesn't seem to be enough either—no success is enough success. You just keep driving yourself, too."

He looked at her a moment, his mouth set uneasily. His gray eyes hardened. Then he laughed. "That's different. I'm not greedy—just sensible. I'd never put a little daughter of mine to work for me, I'll tell you that."

"Wouldn't you?" Dare mused unhappily. "I bet you would for your precious wine."

"No, I wouldn't. And I wouldn't let her carry on the way you do," he drawled, still watching her. "You put on your cowboy boots and run off to play with abandoned dogs. You don't return your business calls, but while the world goes to hell in New York, you teach yourself to make cookies. Cute. If you were my kid, I'd put you over my knee, spank you good, then tell you to stand on your own two feet and face reality."

She sat very straight, very stiff in her chair.

He held out his cup to her for a refill, and she felt like a child pretending to pour at a tea party.

"I know," she said, "you think I have the mental age of eight—"

"I didn't say that," he corrected. "I said you had to postpone your childhood. Nothing wrong with that. Have your fun. God knows that's always been my philosophy."

"I can believe that," she said darkly, forgetting for the moment that if he were a man who lived for fun, he also managed to work very hard.

"So," he said, reaching into his shirt pocket and drawing out a deck of cards, "since fun in the country is low-key, let's get on with your childhood."

He began to shuffle the cards expertly. He handed them to her.

"Now what are you doing?" she asked in genuine puzzlement.

"Ever play cards? Casino, double solitaire, cribbage, spit-in-the-ocean, crazy eights?"

"I never had time," she said, taking the cards.

"Shuffle," he said.

She tried, without much success. "This is silly," she muttered.

"Of course," he said with a mocking smile, "we could get into something else instead. Like the bed. If you decide to grow up, that is. Really declare your independence and then take the chances normal women take. Like with me. I have some fantasies. Want to hear about them?"

"No," she said shortly, trying to hide the unwanted sensations his suggestion raised.

"Then deal," he said grimly.

He taught her to play casino, and then he beat her every game.

"Tomorrow's Sunday," he said as he left. "I'll take the day off. We'll go to the river. I've got a speedboat. I'll teach you to water-ski."

"I'm not athletic," she protested. "I'll probably drown."

"No, you won't," he said, looking into her eyes. "I'll save you. I always do, don't I?"

Then he kissed her good-night, as impersonally as if she were a cousin.

"'Night, Miz Dareen," he said, in his most exaggerated Southern drawl. "I told you we'll have fun, and we will. I'll help you live the childhood you missed—unless you want to grow up, be your own person and take real chances. See, I have these fantasies..."

"I don't want to hear about them," she said curtly. And she didn't. The merest touch of his mouth had filled her with aching dizziness. She was starting to have fantasies of her own.

THE RAIN STOPPED, and the next few days gleamed with sun. They seemed to shine as preciously as gold as they passed, and Dare knew she would always remember them. They had been as close to perfect as anyone could hope for.

She and Rip spent Sunday playing on the river, with an apprehensive Limburger standing watch in the speedboat. Afterward, Rip took her into Arcadia for dinner and a movie. Limburger was not invited. Dare felt more excited than she ever had in Manhattan. She had almost forgotten what a city looked like at night. A few weeks ago Arcadia had seemed tiny. Now it seemed as large as any city ought to be.

Mrs. Bailey had been right. Life on the mountain changed a person. It changed one's perspective. It created a peculiar center of calm, an acute point of reference for knowing what mattered and what did not.

What mattered, Dare realized, was Rip. He mattered as much as the sun and rain mattered to a good harvest. For though he teased her, he was kinder to her than anyone had ever been. He made her laugh when she thought she had forgotten how. If his hints about an affair sometimes nettled her, they also raised a difficult problem. What was he asking, after all, except that she act like the normal and loving woman she was? To take a chance on caring for someone, with no guarantee things between them would last? People took chances like that all the time.

He was honest about it. He was equally honest in not saying he loved her. He only wanted her. She cursed fate for creating a man who was so kind and yet who kept his heart so guarded. Sometimes she thought he really didn't even want her that much anymore, that he had dismissed her as too inexperienced, too troublesome.

Since the night of the storm, he'd treated her blithely, with maddening offhandedness. Still, sometimes she saw him looking at her in a way that made her nerves turn warm and trembling.

He came by every night with some childish game or pastime. Once he'd even brought a portable computer and a computer game.

"Try it," he said, booting up the computer at the kitchen table. "It's a great game—Dragon Trial. A quest, I got it for my nephew when he visits. I'll bet you'll never get past the dragons. Or even the Warlock of the West. He'll turn you into a toad."

Indeed, the Warlock of the West turned her into a toad repeatedly, until Rip told her the secret for getting past him and finding the dragons' lair. Then she couldn't figure out how to outwit the dragons. No matter where she fled, they found her.

"Try facing them," he hinted at last.

The words seemed to settle heavily between them. She knew he was telling her to face the real dragons in her life.

"They're too powerful," she said softly.

"If you say so," he returned. "But you'll never win if you don't." He switched off the game, without giving her a chance to fight the dragons.

He'd laughed about it, and said she missed the entire moral, as usual.

Every night he'd kissed her goodbye with the same nonchalance. Every night she fought the desire to put her arms around his neck and whisper, "Stay."

Then, after he left, she lay in bed, hugging her pillow, remembering his words. He had fantasies. She would ask him to make love to her. And there would be no guarantees. No commitments.

Never, she thought. She would never ask him. Well, maybe, she thought.

No, she assured herself. She couldn't ask. What if that was all he wanted, and then he grew tired of her? That would destroy her. She cared for him too much.

In the meantime, to Rip's surprise, she'd been befriending Stormy, who even let her handle the puppies now. It was like finding twelve new friends. She was inordinately proud of her success with the dogs. Rip shook his head and grinned. "The queen of the modeling world," he said, "and all she really wants to be is a county dog warden." But he'd told her he was proud of her.

Each day, each night, was perfect, she told herself. *No,* she admitted in her heart. *Things were far from perfect.*

Rip treated her as indulgently as he might have treated an underprivileged child. She was both grateful and frustrated—frustrated because she knew she was living in a dream. She was hopelessly in love with him, yes—but she hadn't yet faced the dragons and she knew it was only a matter of time before they caught up with her. She wished the dream could go on forever. She knew it could not.

It ended, with a crash, on a Thursday afternoon so burnished with sunshine that the whole world seemed made of jewels. It seemed an unlikely day for dreams to die.

Rip had stopped by in the morning, as usual. He brought her a strange and exotic-looking flower. It was white and lavender, as lovely and complex as an orchid. "A passion flower," he explained. "They grow wild here. There seem to be more of them since you came to the mountain. What do you suppose that means?"

She said she didn't know.

He laughed and told her she always refused to face her responsibilities. She had made them grow. "I think this whole mountain's in love with you," he'd said, and gave her a brotherly chuck under the chin.

Why couldn't you be? she thought.

After lunch she'd made an emergency trip to Arcadia to buy dog food. She was going through it swiftly, she thought, but then, after all, Stormy was eating for twelve.

She was on the back porch, struggling to pour dog food out of the twenty pound sack into a bucket, when she heard a car stop. Limburger, inside, began barking.

Oh, no, she thought. She hoped Mr. McFee and Mrs. Bailey hadn't returned.

She set down the sack, took up the bucket, and walked around the house to the front. Her feet were bare, and she had to wipe a strand of hair back from her eyes.

An unfamiliar scarlet car gleamed in the afternoon sun.

"Rebecca of Sunnybrook Farm," said a glib, almost girlish voice.

She looked up at the porch in terrified amazement.

It was Sullivan.

He stood by the front door. He was wearing a pink silk shirt, half unbuttoned, and pastel pink pants. Neck chains gleamed against the carefully cultivated tan of his throat. His diamond earring glistened. His famous sapphire eyes were hidden by mirrored sunglasses. His famous blond hair was nearly hidden by a white panama hat.

From inside the house, Limburger barked furiously. Sullivan hit his fist against the screen door with savage suddenness. "Shut up, mutt."

Limburger did not shut up, so Sullivan strolled to the edge of the porch. He looked down at her. Then he smiled the famous white smile.

"Call off your dog, Sheffy. My God, you look dowdy. What have you done to yourself?"

"Nothing," she breathed, still staring up at him in disbelief. He seemed to glitter like a tinsel-decorated Christmas tree.

"That," he said, "seems pretty obvious. Fawn always said you were a peasant at heart. My God, barefoot even. With the milk pail yet. And you've gained weight."

"I'm still underweight," she said uneasily.

"Come on up," Sullivan ordered. "Let me in the house. This heat is killing. This light is killing. I've heard of living in the boondocks, but this is the boondocks that ends all boondocks, honey. Strictly sticks and hicks. Did you actually think this would make you happy?" He laughed unpleasantly.

She set down the pail and went up the stairs shakily. "What do you want?" she asked. Barefoot, she was the same height as he.

"First, inside. Second, a cold drink. Third, for you to stop acting up and to listen to reason. I canceled a concert date for this. I flew from Dallas on a plane made of old orange crates, then rented that damned cheap car, which clashes with my outfit. You've put me to a lot of trouble, Sheffy-doll."

She shushed Limburger, then pushed open the door. "You can come in," she said nervously. "I'll give you a lemonade. Then go. The only thing I want to settle with you is that things are over between us."

He followed her inside. He took off the sunglasses, folded them rather prissily and thrust them into the pocket of his shirt. He turned the full power of his blue eyes on her. She remembered with embarrassment that he wore eye makeup. It didn't seem to matter in New York. Now it struck her as rather sickening.

"Things are not over between us," he said, and examined the room with distaste. "My God," he said. "Look at that love seat. Terminally tacky. It makes me want to puke. What would Fawn say? She'd spin in her grave."

"I'll get you the lemonade," she said tersely. "Then you can go back to wherever you came from."

He flopped down in the green chair, took off the panama hat and shook out his gold locks. He ran his hand through his hair, the rings on his hands sparkling.

He sneezed violently and pulled out a rose-colored silk handkerchief. "I'm allergic to dogs," he said. "Can't you put this thing outside? I've seen rats in New York with better breeding than this hair ball. Good Lord, it's hot. I've been driving for hours. I'm positively limp."

She called Limburger, deposited him on the porch, poured a glass of lemonade and stalked back into the living room.

"Here," she said, thrusting it at Sullivan. "Take it. Then go."

She didn't sit.

He sipped at the lemonade and looked her over from head to foot. He seemed to find what he saw distasteful. His fine nose wrinkled. His artificially darkened brows drew together. "Sit down, you simpleton."

Almost without thinking, she sat down. "Simpleton" had been one of Fawn's favorite warning words. Dare responded to its criticism and its authority automatically.

"We'll talk. Then you start packing," he ordered. "We can get back to Texas and get married tonight. There's no waiting period there."

She looked at him in genuine wonder. She had once thought this man attractive, she told herself in disbelief. This man whose boyish good looks were marred by affectation. He looked as artificial as a plastic flower. His manner was as obnoxious as that of a spoiled child.

She laughed, as much at herself as at him. "Sullivan," she said, "we're not getting married. We were never really engaged. You never paid any attention to me at all. My mother came on practically all of our dates and you always paid more attention to her. The two of you could talk money all night long."

"She was a very smart woman," he returned stonily. "It's hard to believe the two of you are related. We're getting married all right, Shef. The word's out, and it won't hurt either of our careers."

"Careers?" she asked, shaking her head in disbelief. "I've had a career since I was practically a baby. I'm tired of it. People don't get married because of careers. For once in our lives let's be honest, Sullivan. You never liked me very much. And now I don't like you. That's hardly a basis for marriage."

He eyed her coldly. "Tired of your career? Nice. So what do you expect to do?"

She met his stare. "Stay here. I like it here. Take some college courses. Maybe buy a little farm of my own. Grow things. Have animals."

He tossed back his head and laughed, a high-pitched giggle.

"It's not funny," she said, her eyes narrowing.

"It's hysterical. You're hysterical. What do you plan to live on? Air? Your good looks?"

"The money from my trust," she shot back. "I worked years for it—I've hardly seen any of it. Now it's time for me to decide how I want to live my own life."

"Poor little baby Sheffy," he mocked. He pulled out the rose-colored handkerchief again and wiped the sweat from his brow. "You don't have the faintest notion, do you?"

"The faintest notion about what?"

"Have you tried to get hold of Warren lately?"

Her spine stiffened. The air in the room suddenly seemed oppressive. "Yes," she said, her voice edged with tension. "Where is he?"

"Hiding. In South America, I hear. Waiting."

"Waiting for what?"

"To see what you'll do. You've got him scared out of his wits."

"Me?" she asked, her brows rising. "Why should Warren be frightened of me?"

"Because if you don't behave, he's ruined," Sullivan said with a smile of cold satisfaction. "And him with a wife and two kids still in college. For shame, Sheffy. To cause so much misery."

She stood up. "Sullivan, go away," she said. "Stop talking in circles. I can't do anything to Warren. I just want to live my own life."

"You can't," he said, with that same grim smile of satisfaction.

"What?"

"You can't, Shef. There won't be any money to live your own life on. You'll be wiped out unless you do exactly as I say."

She stared down at him, then laughed softly, as if he had made a clever joke. "What?"

"I said, you do exactly as I say. Or you'll be ruined. We all will."

"I don't understand—"

"Fawn fooled with that money in your trust for years, Sheffy," Sullivan said contemptuously. "Even you're not too naive to have missed that. She couldn't stand for anybody else to have control of it. She knew she could make more on her own than any bank or investment company could. They'd play it too conservatively. Fawn had vision, guts and smarts. She was going to take a small fortune and make it into a very large one. Warren was nothing but a front. He never managed your money. She did."

"What are you trying to tell me?" she asked in rising irritation. "Did she lose it? Fine. It never seemed real to me anyway. I still have her estate. She paid herself well out of the money I made."

"You won't have her estate," Sullivan said smoothly. "You won't have a thing. The estate will be gone. Unless you come with me now."

"What are you talking about?" Dare asked desperately. "How do you know all this? Don't answer that. It's obvious. You know because it's about money. Money's all you ever cared about anyway—just leave me alone. I don't want to marry you. You don't want to marry me."

"You're right, Sheffy. I don't want to marry you," he said. His voice was calm, but she thought he looked pale beneath his tan. "I never did want to. It wasn't you I wanted. That's why—" He wiped his forehead with the square of silk again. "I—I married Fawn, Sheffy. I married your mother. In Mexico. Last spring."

Dare felt as if she'd been struck. She could get no air. She felt sick. Her knees went weak. *No,* she thought. *No. I did not hear him say that.*

"What?" she asked helplessly.

"When I was down making that video and you were shooting the jewelry ads. All right. We were a little drunk. But we thought we might as well be hung for sheep as lambs. Afterward we wondered if we'd been stupid. But we didn't get to wonder long. A week and a half later she had that first stroke," he explained. He stared up at her impassively, as if he was describing the weather.

She could only stare back at him, wondering if she was going to be sick.

"Sit down," he sneered. "You look even more awful than when I got here. You wanted honesty? All right, you've got it. Look, Shef, we didn't mean to hurt anybody. Especially you. We'd have told you eventually. We'd have figured out something."

She sank to the love seat. She stared at him as if hypnotized. "You were in love with my mother the whole time?" she asked weakly. "You were engaged to me, and you were in love with my mother?"

He leaned over and took her cold hand between his sweaty ones. She drew away. He shrugged and let her.

"She and I, we were two of a kind. Her, from that rat hole mining town, me from the streets of Pittsburgh—we knew what poverty was. We knew what ambition was. We understood each other...she wasn't that much older than me. She was forty. I'm almost thirty-one, if you want to know the truth..."

Dare began to laugh softly. She had never heard anything so funny in her life. Her own fiancé had been married to her mother—and he wasn't twenty-four. He was almost thirty-one.

"Stop it!" he ordered. He reached over, grabbed her blouse front and yanked, hard. Then he released her.

"Stop laughing. It's not what you think. We—we were soul mates, her and me. I always preferred older women. Always. But age didn't matter—like I said, we were two of a kind. Nobody ever knew what we were thinking. But we knew. We knew each other down to the bone. And she was so bright about your career, my career, money—"

She laughed again. "Of course! The money—always the money—"

He rose, stood over her. He gripped her by the shoulder, shaking her into silence. "Shut up and listen. You don't remember what it's like to be poor. I do. So did Fawn. She made sure that you had everything. Everything. But we wanted to make sure we all got the best of everything, and so we started a company—Saji: Sheffield and Johns, Incorporated. We knew we'd make millions, Sheffy—we knew it."

"You two did something crooked, didn't you?" she asked, tears stinging her eyes. She wasn't sure if they were tears of laughter or pain, and only Sullivan's cruel grip on her shoulder kept her from laughing again. "You did something illegal, and now it's caught up with you—hasn't it?"

"Listen, you spoiled brat," he said, giving her another shake. "Almost every dime I have is in Saji—and every dime you have, too—so it's no laughing matter. All right—it was illegal. We were partners, and Warren fronted for us. We were using your trust money—and Warren knew. He had a piece of the action too. He got his cut. He knew he stood to make a bundle for himself...."

She stared up at him. She ran the back of her hand across her eyes to wipe the tears away. "Come out with it, Sullivan," she baited him. "Just how deep does it go?"

"All the way," he said between his teeth. "All that money is in Saji—but there really is no Saji. It was just a phantom company. We used it as a front. All its assets went into my company—SullCo. Into the recording studio. Into the records I'm producing. I'm hot, Sheffy. I'm very hot. All your trust money is invested in me. And all Fawn's money. And some of Warren's. And a lot of other shareholders who don't know what Saji really is, but stand to make a lot of money from it. We were going to blow the lid off the entertainment industry. We were all going to be rich. But then she died."

"And then she died," she said bitterly, wiping her hand across her eyes again. "Now you're telling me she lied to me? You lied to me? Warren lied to me? All for some stupid *company*?"

"Not stupid, smart," he hissed, gripping her shoulder more tightly. "Can't you understand that? All right. We shouldn't have got married. But it was like we could do no wrong. It was like *destiny*. It was like being drunk on power—our one mistake. But if the truth about the marriage comes out, my career is ruined. Worse, my company is ruined. And so are you and I and Warren and a bunch of other people. If Saji is investigated, all the garbage about the phony company and siphoning the funds and manipulating your trust fund will come out. And there are—well—a few fast moves we pulled on the IRS. Warren and I will be up before a grand jury. Unless—unless we can keep this all in the family, so to speak—"

"The family?" she repeated, beginning to feel hysterical. "Some family—I don't even understand what you're saying, except I know it's dishonest—"

"Shut up! It's simple. We formed Saji to get money for SullCo. We wanted to put the money where the action was. Fawn and I had joint tenancy. But people are becoming suspicious, Dare. Fawn and I weren't exactly discreet in Mexico. There's a Mexican reporter after this story, and he's getting too close for comfort. One thing leads to another. First they'll find out about Fawn and me. Then they'll wonder why we were doing business together.... The whispers have started. There's only one way to stop them—you and I get married.''

"Married? How does that help this whole miserable mess?'' she demanded tearfully.

"If you marry me, the rumors about Fawn and me would stop. We have time to cover up everything. It's getting bad enough that the *World Sun* is beginning to smell something. But if you don't cooperate—and if it comes out—everything crumbles. We end up in ruins. My name is mud and so is Warren's. You're pulled in, too— guilt by association. So all we have to do is get married, Sheffy. It'd stop any rumors about me and Fawn. Family business stays family business. We make our fortune and then we get out of it—go to Switzerland, South America. You get rich, I get rich, what harm is there in that?''

"Harm?'' she cried. "Marry you? To cover up the fact that you lied and cheated and embezzled? Are you insane?''

"You used to like me,'' he said, staring at her through his lashes. She realized he was giving her his sultry look. "Look, who's gonna believe any of this stuff if you and I get married? Would you marry a man who jilted you for your mother? Would you marry a man who dipped into your trust fund? Of course not! You put the rumors to sleep. You give me time to fix things up. We both get incredible publicity—America's sweethearts wed at last. Everything's fine. My career goes on, and you've got a big piece of the action.''

She stood up again. "You're not even human," she said numbly.

He moved to her, standing close. He put his hands on her arms. She shivered with revulsion, but didn't have the strength to strike his hands away.

"You and my mother," she said, still dazed. "My own mother—"

"Wasn't she supposed to have any happiness of her own, Sheffy?" he asked persuasively. "I made her happy. I told you. We didn't do it to hurt you. We would have taken care of you. We always took care of you."

She looked in his painted eyes, stunned.

"She loved you," he wheedled. "The whole Saji thing was for you, too. To make sure you got full benefit from your money. But if all this ever comes out—what are people going to say about her? Think about it. Marry me—or her reputation goes down in history as one of the great American con-women. And yours goes down as one of the great wide-eyed dupes."

"You pretend you loved her," she said. "You didn't even come see her when she was sick." She shook her head angrily. "And as if I cared what anybody thought about me at this point—" she began, her mind hazy. All she could think of was how evil Sullivan's warm, soft hands felt.

"I couldn't stand to see her that way, Sheffy," he crooned. "It hurt me too much. Besides, I didn't want to foster any rumors. And she and I—we had something most people never even dream of. You couldn't understand that. It was more than sex. It was power. Pure power."

"Power," she muttered in disgust. She shook her head to clear it.

"Yes. Power. Don't sound so righteous. If you don't want to think about yourself," he coaxed, "think about Warren—his wife, his kids. Think about me. People depend on me. The members of my band haven't been as careful about their money as I have. And what about the people who take a financial dive if Saji crashes? Tiffany, for instance. Vernon's secretary. Fawn gave her a hot stock tip. Tiffany's got her entire savings invested in me and she doesn't even know it. You want to hurt her? Hurt all of them? Of course not. So do as I say. It's just a marriage. It's nothing personal."

She thought of Warren, his wife, his children and the members of Sullivan's band, Brian, Hondo and Jack. Sullivan's staff. Then the image of her mother's face flashed before her vividly—laughing, foxlike, driven. Fawn, who never felt safe. Had she felt safe at last with Sullivan?

"I can't leave here," Dare said. In her mind her answer was almost logical. "I have dogs to take care of."

The moist hands tightened on her arms. "You really are a simpleton," he said between clenched teeth. "Who cares about the damned dogs? We've got millions of dollars at stake here! Reputations! Lives! I'm trying to talk to you about the real world, damn it."

The real world, she thought wildly. She had tried to escape the real world. She could not. It had come after her. If she tried to escape it again, she would have nothing—except the responsibility for ruining the lives of dozens of people.

Again she thought of Warren's family, of the people around Sullivan. She thought of scandal, mammoth scandal, that would shake both the entertainment industry and the business world. How many people would be hurt before it was over? And how many would be destroyed?

"Pack," Sullivan ordered.

She stared at him, his perfect tan, his pale gold hair, his painted eyes.

"We can get married tonight," he said smoothly. "Then we'll all be safe. Come on, Sheffy. It's the only answer. Fawn would have known that. If she were here, she'd tell you to do it. In a few years we get a divorce. You're rich, I'm rich, everybody's rich. You can marry whoever you want. You can buy whoever you want."

She knew the man she wanted wouldn't have her if she did that. The man she wanted couldn't be bought.

"Come on, Sheffy," he whispered. He kissed her cheek.

She shuddered, but allowed him. It was as if her destiny had claimed her.

"Pack," he repeated, and kissed her cheek again. He smelled like perfume. "You don't want to see Warren in jail, do you? You don't want to see a bunch of people lose their life savings. You don't want the world to misunderstand your mother. She worked so hard. She deserves to rest in peace."

Rip, she thought. *Walk through the door and save me.*

But no one came. There was only Sullivan.

"I'll have to do something about the dogs," she said numbly.

"Fine," he said, and smiled with satisfaction.

"And Sheffy," he said, still smiling. "Don't worry. I'll take care of you."

CHAPTER TEN

WHICH WORLD WAS REAL? she wondered with uneasy dreaminess as she got ready. Sullivan's or Rip's?

Sullivan's, answered a cynical voice deep within her.

Already she could feel Sullivan's reality closing around her like a curtain. When she peeked through the curtain, the little farmhouse looked dim, insubstantial. The mountains seemed to be disappearing, the sunshine fading.

Already she remembered the hectic rhythm of Manhattan and her blood raced desperately to its hard drumming.

At Sullivan's request, she masked her face with makeup, as in the old days. She glued on the false eyelashes. She put on the only dress she'd brought, a simple white linen one she had worn into Arcadia with Rip.

She looked at her reflection moodily. A stranger looked back—a weirdly familiar one. The girl Fawn had invented had taken over Dare's body once more. She had taken over her life.

She should have known there was no escape. She thought of Rip, and the memory of him filled her with utter longing and regret.

She wished he would come and save her—come and help her the way he'd done before. But she knew he wouldn't, he'd told her she was on her own. Wasn't that what she wanted?

Besides, he'd tried to save her all along, she realized numbly. She hadn't let him. Now it was too late.

"Hurry up," snapped Sullivan's voice from the living room. "I want out of this shack."

She came out of the bedroom. She looked at him. Yes, he was there, and all too real.

"You'll have to drive that mutt wherever you're taking him by yourself," he said, fanning through a copy of *Billboard*. "I'm not putting him in my car. I'll sneeze all the way to Dallas."

"I'll take him," she said. She got Limburger's leash from its hook. She scribbled a note of explanation to Rip:

> I have to go away. I'm marrying Sullivan after all.
> Please watch out for Limburger. Make sure nothing
> happens to the dogs in the barn. I'll send you a
> check for their keep. Thanks for everything—Dare.

How stupid, she thought. The note said nothing. "Thanks for everything" was so trite. She should have thanked him for the most wonderful time of her life—a time that would have to last her the rest of her life. And for being the only person in her life that was decent and caring. And for touching her, holding her so that she turned from stone into flesh.

She got into the Chevy and drove to Rip's place. She had never seen his house before. It was a big, beautiful house of native stone, sitting high on the mountain. The front yard was filled with magnolia trees.

She would leave the dog and the note with Tessie. Rip would be in the fields. At least she wouldn't have to put herself through the pain of saying goodbye. She knocked. Nobody answered the door.

She looked around. The view here was even more spectacular than from her porch. The day was hot and bright and blue, and every detail of the mountains in the distance seemed preternaturally clear.

At last she tied the long leash to the railing of the porch door and placed the note under Limburger's collar. He began to yelp in protest as she walked away. The farther away she got, the louder he yelped. He danced and strained at the leash, trying to follow her.

Don't look back, she warned herself, fighting off on-coming tears. *Don't listen, don't look. Go into your dreamworld, where you used to go when things got hard.* She bit her lip, got in the car and drove away, Limburger's cries still ringing in her head. She thought, I won't start crying, because if I do, I'll never quit.

"I'll have to stop in Arcadia," she told Sullivan when she got back to the house. "I'll have to turn in my key to the agent and explain."

"Mail the key," Sullivan said shortly. "To hell with explanations."

"I want to stop," she said with such firmness that he blinked in surprise. "I want everything to be rounded out, to come full circle. I remember the day I got the key. I want to remember handing it back. The day it started, the day it ended."

He looked at her lazily. "What's the matter, Sheffy?" he asked, amused. "You fall for one of the local boys? Some guy on a tractor? That would be about your style. God, it's a good thing I came around to save you from yourself."

"I want to stop in Arcadia," she repeated, trying not to think of Rip. But she thought of him anyway—his gray eyes, strong arms, his easy smile. Now all he meant was lost laughter. Lost chances. Lost everything. She should have made love with him—commitments or none. At least she could have had the memory....

"All right," Sullivan agreed pettishly. "Consider it your wedding present. And don't expect anything else. This little side trip to get you has been expensive. I had to cancel a performance. Do you know how much that cost me?"

SULLIVAN DROVE the red car up to McFee's Peerless Realty.

"Make it fast," he ordered. "I don't want to sit here in this heat. And this damned light. It makes my contacts feel like they're pinching my eyes out. God, what a place. Hicksville."

She got out of the car, walked mechanically into the office.

Oliver McFee looked up at her, his old eyes widening in surprise. He took in her makeup, her false eyelashes, with malicious pleasure.

"Well, well, the cover girl," he said. "Nobody could fail to recognize you now."

"I came to turn in my key. I'm leaving," she said without any preliminaries. She wanted to get this over, fast.

"She's leaving. I knew she'd be leaving," said another voice.

Dare blinked in surprise. She hadn't seen Mrs. Bailey, sitting ghostlike and hunched in the corner.

"Oh!" Dare said.

"Leaving? We were just coming to see you," Mr. McFee complained. "It occurred to Mrs. Bailey that we should check the property to see if the storm had done any damage. Insurance claims, et cetera, et cetera."

"I'm leaving," Dare said. "Don't worry. I'm not asking for the rest of the rent back. You can keep it."

"I certainly hope we will keep it," Mr. McFee said with some spirit. "You signed an agreement—"

Mrs. Bailey sat, more wizened than Dare remembered her, her hand on her gold-headed cane. The other hand stroked the rope of pearls that gleamed around her aged throat.

"Look at you," Mrs. Bailey said with satisfaction. "A person cannot see your real face any longer. Do you still have a real face?"

Dare looked into the old woman's strange eyes. "No," she said simply. "I don't."

"Ha!" chortled Mrs. Bailey. "I saw him. I saw him when you drove up. He doesn't have a real face either. But he has money. Lots of money. I can still tell."

In spite of the day's heat and the stuffiness of the office, Mrs. Bailey was making Dare feel cold, chilled.

She handed Mr. McFee the key to the farmhouse. "I've left my car and a few things there," she said. "I'll call someone to deal with them later."

"It goes around and it goes around," said Mrs. Bailey in a bizarre tone. "Power and rumor. Money and love. It goes around like a wheel."

"Mrs. Bailey—please," hissed Mr. McFee.

He squinted at Dare. "Never mind her," he whispered. "It's one of those spells she gets. Pay her no mind. I'm the one you deal with. I protect her business interests."

"Do pay me mind!" said Mrs. Bailey with sudden imperiousness. "Oliver, do you think I am deaf as well as old and tired? I am not. I have earned the right to enjoy myself as I like. And I want to look for a moment at this girl who no longer has a real face."

"I think I should be going," Dare said hastily.

"I wondered what would happen this time," Mrs. Bailey said, her voice aquiver. "The same thing happened. Things never change. They just go around and around."

"I really must—"

"I was far more beautiful than you," said the old woman with surprising force. "And younger. I lived on that mountain once. The property belonged to my uncle then. I spent one perfect summer there. It has had to last me through a lifetime of winter. I hope it will last you, my dear."

"Out, out," said Mr. McFee, with a shooting glance at Dare. "You upset her for some reason. Be gone and good riddance. I'll check out the property and send you a bill for any damage."

"So you, too, were fated to come," laughed Mrs. Bailey, looking at Dare with malicious delight. "And you, too, are leaving. For an unwholesome young man with money. You think he will guarantee your future? He will, he will. Look at me, miss. I am your future. I am what you will be."

"Tabitha! Please!" remonstrated Mr. McFee. "I don't want to have to call Dr. Glossit! My good woman, get hold of yourself. That was fifty years ago!"

"It was yesterday!" cried Mrs. Bailey. She jerked at the pearls so hard the string broke. The pearls rained to the floor and began to roll wildly.

"It was yesterday!" she said again in a voice of strange despair. "I left the mountain and Homais DuLong yesterday, and the enchantment broke. I ended up with Robert E. Lee Bailey and all his money could buy. The mountain and the wine called me back, but it was too late. Too late!"

The woman began to laugh wildly. Mr. McFee looked rather wild himself, and began to scuttle around the room, chasing the pearls. "Go!" he ordered Dare. "Can't you see what you're doing to her?"

"She's doing nothing to me," laughed Mrs. Bailey, tears in her eyes. "I did it all to myself."

"Go!" shrieked Mr. McFee. He had one hand filled with pearls and with the other he seized a real estate brochure and began to fan Mrs. Bailey.

"Yes," said Mrs. Bailey, laughing so hard there were tears in her eyes. "Go! But never deceive yourself that the DuLong man will miss you. He won't. They aren't like other people. They don't understand regret. Not at all. Not one of them."

Dare fled.

Sullivan drove like a madman, and they just made their flight to Dallas.

DARE SAT in the Manhattan apartment the next week, the papers scattered around her. Their names—hers and Sullivan's were everywhere.

She looked at the photograph of herself and Sullivan on the garish cover of the *World Sun*.

"What have I done?" she asked herself miserably. She threw herself across the double bed and cried aloud. "Did I do the right thing? I did what I had to. Didn't I?"

SHE SIGHED WITH FATIGUE as she drove the rented car into the sleepy little Southern town.

The sign at the city limits said Arcadia. Population: 4,126 Nice Folks and A Few Old Grouches. And Some Darn Good Hound Dogs.

She stopped at the real estate office to pick up the key to the farmhouse. Mr. McFee told her that Mrs. Bailey had had a breakdown, so Dare stopped at the hospital to see her, but the old woman was resting. She was going to be fine, the nurse said. She was acting almost sweet-natured these days. Not quite, but almost. It was as if some fever that had gripped her for years had finally broken.

She drove out of Arcadia and higher into the mountains. The oak and pine forests fell away, and the rolling vineyards began.

She willed the protesting car to climb DuLong's mountain. The western sky was beginning to burn pink and gold with the sunset.

She stopped the car before the tall native stone house. Her heart tightened.

She got out of the car almost fearfully. She wore the same khaki shorts and plain shirt she had worn on her first trip to the mountain. Her hair was loose and flowing. She wore no makeup.

She knocked hesitantly at the front door. It felt like a year before it opened.

Rip stood in the doorway, tall, gray-eyed, a lock of hair falling over his forehead.

"So," he said, no laughter in his eyes. "You're back."

"Yes," she breathed, looking up at him. "I'm back. For a little while."

Limburger, hearing her voice, began to throw himself madly at the screen door. Rip opened it. The dog ran out and she scooped him up with desperate affection. "Come on in," Rip said impersonally.

They went into the living room. It was a huge room, with a deep forest-green carpet as thick as velvet, mullioned windows, and a towering fireplace made of native stone.

"Thank you for taking care of him," Dare said nervously, clutching Limburger close to her.

Rip's eyes held hers. "You're welcome."

"How are the other dogs? Stormy and the pups?"

"Fine." His gaze didn't waver. "Did you come all this way to talk about dogs?"

"No."

The tension stretching between them seemed unbearable to her. "Did you get the harvest in?"

"Yes. Did you come all this way to talk about the harvest?"

"No." Her eyes wavered from his. She hugged the dog more tightly and looked at the floor. "You never called," she said at last.

"No," he said. He went to a cabinet and took out a bottle of port. "But I sent you a note of congratulation. I thought maybe you'd read between the lines. Want a drink?" he asked.

"No." She stood watching him, her heart beating fast.

"I think I need one," he said. He filled a small glass and tossed it off, faster than he should have. "So you did it, did you?" he asked at last, staring at her from across the room. "I didn't think you would."

"I had to," she said. Her chest seemed so tight now that she couldn't get her breath.

He smiled ironically. He poured himself another glass of port. He toasted her. "To you."

"It wasn't easy for me," she tried to explain.

"I don't suppose it was," he observed, then sipped the port. "How does it feel?"

"It feels—just fine, I guess," she said.

She put Limburger down. "Oh, Rip, talk to me. Say something. It's all been so hard."

He set down the glass. He put his hands in the back pockets of his jeans. He stared out the window at the sunset. "I know it has. But I'm proud of you. What you did took courage. And, if the truth be told, I'm glad you're back. Even for a little while."

"I—I got as far as Dallas with him," she said, the story beginning to pour out breathlessly. "But I couldn't go through with it. I think it was Mrs. Bailey—seeing Mrs. Bailey like that—"

"Mrs. Bailey?" he asked with a crooked smile. "Somehow I hoped it might have something to do with me."

"Oh, Rip, listen," she said. "I was pulled two ways. I didn't want to leave here. But I was afraid of how many people I could hurt if I didn't. But I couldn't go through with it. I knew it was wrong. So while Sullivan was in the shower, I called the authorities in New York, and I told them everything—about the trust, the marriage, Saji. Then I took a plane back to Manhattan. There are some people who will never forgive me."

"Indeed, there are," he said, cocking an eyebrow. "And how does that feel?"

"Not very good at all," she confessed. "The only thing that takes the load off my shoulders is that Warren broke first. He'd already told them. He phoned from South America. He couldn't take the pressure any longer. But I didn't know that when I called."

"So you finally faced the dragons, eh?" he asked casually.

"Yes," she said softly. "I thought you'd call."

"I couldn't," he said simply. He still stared out at the sunset.

"Why?"

"At first I thought you'd really gone off and married that little reptile. God. Then when the story—the real story hit the papers, I realized what had happened. That you'd finally made your choice. With no help from anybody at all."

He turned and smiled at her. "I was proud of you, Dare. I am proud of you. You did what you had to do. And I tried to give you a gift."

"A gift?" she asked dubiously.

He took the wineglass and raised it to her again. "The gift of letting you do it alone. I figured if you wanted help from me, you'd ask for it. But you didn't. You didn't need me. You didn't need anybody. I was always afraid you were weak. You proved you were strong. I didn't interfere."

She looked at him questioningly.

He set his jaw. He shrugged one wide shoulder. "From the moment I met you, you were trying so hard to take care of yourself. To be independent. People had been telling you what to do for too long."

"You think going through this alone was easy?" she asked, wondering what he meant. Was he just going to stand there and moralize? Didn't he care about what she had gone through, or that she had come back!

"You think letting you go through it alone was easy?" he snapped back. "My God, I didn't sleep nights thinking what you must be feeling. For the first time in my life I drank too much. Me! I grew up surrounded by thousands of barrels of wine, and for the first time in my life I was tempted to get drunker than Bacchus himself."

"But why didn't you call?" she asked in a small voice.

"I told you." His voice was strained. "Because you didn't ask for my help. This was something you had to do on your own. You have an unfortunate talent, my dear.

You make people want to take care of you. You made me want to take care of you. But slowly I realized that if you were ever going to respect yourself, if you were ever going to be allowed to grow up, there had to be a moment when nobody took care of you—except you."

She studied his face in the fading golden light.

"They say," he remarked stonily. "If you love something, set it free. If it comes back, it's yours. If it doesn't, it never was. I was trying to dominate you, Dare. I know I was. It was because I was worried as hell about you. But that wasn't what you wanted at that point in your life. And it wasn't what you needed. So I let you go it alone. You can forgive me or not."

"Well," she said, lifting her chin. "I stood on my own two feet."

"And did a fine job of it," he said crisply.

"And you set me free," she went on, a catch in her voice.

"And did an equally fine job of it."

"Well," she gulped. "You set me free. But I came back."

He set down his glass. He looked at her hard from across the room. "So you did."

"Rip DuLong," she said in sudden frustration. "I went through sheer misery without you!"

He was across the room in two strides. He crushed her in his arms and kissed her with a passion she'd never known.

"I was giving you another week," he muttered, kissing her cheek, her temple, her hair. "Then I was coming to New York after you. I'd have dragged you back here where you belong by your beautiful hair. Independence is independence, but enough is enough."

"I didn't know if you really cared if I came back," she said huskily, winding her arms around his neck. "I mean you always teased, you were never serious about that."

"Listen," he said, then kissed her lower lip, nibbling it until she was breathless. "If I got any more serious about you, I'd be dead. From the moment I saw you—lamp shade and all—I suddenly understood why God put me on this green earth—*to love you*. But there was the matter of a fiancé standing between us. And my own damned hardheadedness. And the fact you had to do all your growing up in such a short time."

"I'm here without asking for any promises," she said, half laughing as she clung to him. "What I felt for you frightened me. But I've come back for as long as you want me. I'm grown up now. I'm willing to take chances."

He groaned, squeezing her closer to him. "Oh, Dare, I didn't know how much I wanted you until I thought you were gone. I kept telling myself I didn't want to marry anybody—and like a fool I kept telling you, because I was fighting what I felt. From the moment I saw you, I wanted you and I wanted you forever. I just couldn't admit it."

"Oh, Rip—" she said, dizzied by his passion.

"Dare, maybe I've learned to take chances myself. What you said that night was right. I'd driven myself to the point where no success was enough. I let my parents' mistakes almost let me make a huge one of my own. But you belong here. You belong with me. Marry me. This damned mountain doesn't mean a thing with you gone. It's nothing but stone and earth and vines without you. Say you'll marry me. Say it."

"Yes," she said between kisses. "But I'm practically poor now. If I stay, you will have to take care of me."

"With pleasure, my dear," he said, kissing her throat. "With pleasure that I hope is mutual. And lifelong."

"The lawyers say they can get some of the money back, but—"

"Oh, stop talking about money," he whispered against her throat.

She drew away from him momentarily and gave his face a searching look. "I might never have had the nerve if it hadn't been for Mrs. Bailey, Rip. Were she and your grandfather in love?"

"Mrs. Bailey again?" he growled. "Do I get no credit at all that you're back here in my arms?"

"Oh, you know better than that," she said affectionately. "But were they? She talked as if they were and she'd left him, and that she'd hated herself her whole life for it."

"Yes," he said with a solemnity foreign to him. "She was under pressure from her father to marry old man Bailey. He was the banker in Arcadia. She thought of the hard life here on the mountain, and the soft life there in town. She made her choice. She was miserable. It's a sad story. But maybe some good came out of it, after all these years."

"And your grandfather?"

"He found a pretty little French-American girl. I don't think he ever forgot Tabitha Bailey. Never forgave her, either. But he got over her. That's probably what embittered her most of all."

"Would you," she asked shyly, "have got over me?"

"No," he answered gruffly. "And don't ever ask again."

"And you think I can really be a country girl?" she teased.

"Honey, you were born one. I used to watch your eyes shine when you'd look out over the mountains. Or the way your face would light up even when you looked at something ordinary—the sumac, the mist in the valley. You were made for this life. You're home here, finally home."

"Oh, Rip," she whispered. "I'm going to be connected to scandal for a while. People will talk."

"It wasn't your doing, love. People will understand."

"And my mother," she said awkwardly, "they'll talk about that."

"Let them talk. Whatever else she did, she gave the world one flawless and wonderful thing—you."

"And I'll probably go on collecting stray dogs...."

"A fine community service," he said, nuzzling her ear. "One that's been sorely lacking. You'll fulfill a desperate need. Now be quiet and kiss me. We've only got a lifetime left. Let's make the most of it. Did I ever mention I had fantasies about you? Do you want me to tell you about them?"

"No," she said against his lips. "Don't tell me. Show me."

"My dear," he breathed. "Just remember. You asked for it. You finally asked for it."

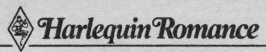
Harlequin Romance

Coming Next Month

2857 A MAN OF CONTRASTS Claudia Jameson
All signs point to a successful union when business owner
Elaine marries a widower with a small son. When she becomes
convinced he's still in love with his first wife, she faces the
future with dismay!

2858 KING OF THE HILL Emma Goldrick
Marcie regards the Adirondacks mountain cabin she inherited
as a needed resting place, until she becomes involved in a
family feud started by her late uncle. Even worse, she fights
with the one man she could love.

2859 VOYAGE OF DISCOVERY Hilda Nickson
Tha Canary Islands cruise is a new experience for Gail—a
pleasant shipboard romance would top it off. But falling in
love is a waste of time when the man in mind is not only
uninterested but engaged!

2860 THE LOVE ARTIST Valerie Parv
Carrie sees famous cartoonist Roger as fancy-free and
irresponsible, just like her father, who'd abandoned his family
to pursue art. No way will she consider Roger as a husband.

2861 RELATIVE STRANGERS Jessica Steele
Zarah travels to Norway to unravel the mystery surrounding
her real mother. She is shocked when she is regarded as a gold
digger even by the one man she can turn to for help—and love.

2862 LOVE UPON THE WIND Sally Stewart
Jenny's quiet London life is disrupted when her lawyer boss's
divorced son asks her to be his secretary. His second request is
even more shattering—to be the wife he needs as a respectable
candidate for Parliament!

Available in August wherever paperback books are sold, or
through Harlequin Reader Service.

In the U.S.
901 Fuhrmann Blvd.
P.O. Box 1397
Buffalo, N.Y. 14240-1397

In Canada
P.O. Box 603
Fort Erie, Ontario
L2A 5X3

In August
Harlequin celebrates

The 1000th

Presents

Passionate Relationship

by
Penny Jordan

**Harlequin Presents,
still and always the No. 1 romance
series in the world!**

Available wherever paperback books are sold.